SWING TIME

"Deke, you can't do this. You know I didn't do nothing wrong."

"It ain't my job to make that decision, it's the judge's. You know that."

The rope chewed into One-Thumb's neck. Its dry, rough edge peeled away the top layers of skin. Feeling the noose dig a little deeper, One-Thumb struggled to straighten his back so he could take one last, gasping breath.

"You know he's wrong, Deke! The judge is—"

It was a short drop, but it was all that was needed. The rope creaked as One-Thumb started to swing in the strong breeze. He swung even more once one of the men slapped something against his chest.

Tacks held a piece of parchment onto the body as if the dead man's torso was just another empty section of wall. All it said was:

LAWBREAKER

HUNG FOR HIS MISDEEDS

BY THE ORDER OF

JUDGE H. KRUEGER

It wasn't much as far as epitaphs go, but it made its point well enough.

THE GUNSMITH
278
THE HANGING JUDGE

J. R. ROBERTS

JOVE BOOKS, NEW YORK

THE BERKLEY PUBLISHING GROUP
Published by the Penguin Group
Penguin Group (USA) Inc.
375 Hudson Street, New York, New York 10014, USA
Penguin Group (Canada), 10 Alcorn Avenue, Toronto, Ontario M4V 3B2, Canada
(a division of Pearson Penguin Canada Inc.)
Penguin Books Ltd., 80 Strand, London WC2R 0RL, England
Penguin Group Ireland, 25 St. Stephen's Green, Dublin 2, Ireland (a division of Penguin Books Ltd.)
Penguin Group (Australia), 250 Camberwell Road, Camberwell, Victoria 3124, Australia
(a division of Pearson Australia Group Pty. Ltd.)
Penguin Books India Pvt. Ltd., 11 Community Centre, Panchsheel Park, New Delhi—110 017, India
Penguin Group (NZ), Cnr. Airborne and Rosedale Roads, Albany, Auckland 1310, New Zealand
(a division of Pearson New Zealand Ltd.)
Penguin Books (South Africa) (Pty.) Ltd., 24 Sturdee Avenue, Rosebank, Johannesburg 2196, South
Africa

Penguin Books Ltd., Registered Offices: 80 Strand, London WC2R 0RL, England

This is a work of fiction. Names, characters, places, and incidents either are the product of the author's imagination or are used fictitiously, and any resemblance to actual persons, living or dead, business establishments, events, or locales is entirely coincidental.

THE HANGING JUDGE

A Jove Book / published by arrangement with the author

PRINTING HISTORY
Jove edition / February 2005

Copyright © 2005 by Robert J. Randisi.

ISBN: 0-515-13889-4

JOVE®
Jove Books are published by The Berkley Publishing Group,
a division of Penguin Group (USA) Inc.
375 Hudson Street, New York, New York 10014.
JOVE is a registered trademark of Penguin Group (USA) Inc.
The "J" design is a trademark belonging to Penguin Group (USA) Inc.

PRINTED IN THE UNITED STATES OF AMERICA

10 9 8 7 6 5 4 3 2 1

ONE

"But I didn't do it! I swear to God!"

The words rolled over the flat prairie like smoke. They spewed forth from heat and fire, but didn't affect a single thing they touched. Instead, they broke apart and dissipated upon stoic faces and uncaring ears. For all the good they did, they might as well not have even existed.

But that didn't mean the words stopped coming. Much like smoke, or even plenty of other folks' words for that matter, they kept right on coming. The man who spoke them was tall, lanky and had a full head of thick, tangled hair. His face was covered in dark whiskers and his eyes were wide and darted disturbingly back and forth.

"Ask anyone around here," the wild-eyed man said. "They'll tell you. For Christ's sake, just give me a chance!"

Of the four men gathered around the one who was doing all the talking, only one of them looked the first fellow directly in the face. That man looked into those wild, daring eyes hard enough to make up for the other three. His own eyes looked like pieces of polished coal behind narrow slits. The line of his mouth was straight and almost completely hidden beneath a thick, well-manicured mustache.

"You had your chance," the man with the narrowed eyes said. "Now it's time to pay your dues."

"Pay? Pay for what?"

"You know goddamn well what you did."

The man with the wild eyes stood with ropes tied around his ankles and wrists. He wore clothes that were nothing more than rags. Blood had soaked into the material so much that it seemed as if the shirt and pants had simply changed color.

Those rags fluttered in the breezes that frequently blew over the flat ground, whistling through the branches of the trees that marked the spot where all five men were gathered. Without much of anything to stop them, the winds were able to gather up plenty of momentum, as well as a voice that sounded like a shrill, sorrowful cry.

With the rope so tightly wrapped around his arms and legs, standing upright was a challenge for the wild-eyed man. If not for the noose tied around his neck, he would have certainly fallen over.

One of those winds came racing by, tugging at the loose corners of the wild-eyed man's shirt and causing him to teeter as if pushed by an invisible hand. Feeling that, his eyes stopped moving and fixed upon a spot directly in front of him so he could concentrate. Once he'd regained his balance, he turned his gaze over to the only other man who was paying him any mind whatsoever.

"How long have we known each other, Deke?" the wild-eyed man asked. "How many times have we swapped stories over a beer?"

Deke stood unmoving, no matter how strong the winds around him got. "It's been a while," he said, the motion of his lips barely visible beneath the thick, drooping curl of his whiskers.

"Then you know this ain't right. You know I wouldn't do anything to warrant dying like this."

The other three men were going about their own tasks

slowly and methodically. Each of them was dressed in a similar fashion to Deke: long, black coats; white shirts; black pants. The only thing to tell them apart was the differing styles of their black hats.

One of these remaining three perked up when he heard what the wild-eyed man had said. "You don't want to die like this, One-Thumb? Then how would you rather die? I'm sure we can spare a bullet if it'll save us the work of hauling your ass up with that rope."

One-Thumb's eyes were still wide open, but now they were no longer so wild. Instead, they took on a pleading, soulful depth. They were the eyes of a man who could just make out the approaching figure of Death. "How about old age? I'll die like that without another word."

The man who'd asked for the suggestion appeared to be the youngest of the bunch. His skin had been made rough as much from hard living as from being just plain ugly. While he had plenty of whiskers sprouting from his face, it seemed unlikely that he would ever get much of a beard or mustache.

The youngest dropped the end of rope he'd been tying down and started walking toward the man attached to the other end. Drawing his pistol, he said, "You got a real smart mouth. How about if I fill it up so's you can't talk no more?"

Before another word could be said, Deke reached out and grabbed hold of the younger man's wrist. His fingers clamped in place like bands of steel and he did so without so much as taking his eyes from One-Thumb's face.

"Ease up, Spencer," Deke said. "No need to make this go any harder than it already is."

The younger man, bristling at having been called by his formal name, stopped himself before saying anything back to Deke. Although he seemed more than anxious to give One-Thumb another piece of his mind, he wasn't half as eager to talk back to Deke.

The remaining two men stopped what they were doing as well. One was writing something on a large piece of parchment and the other was fussing with the noose itself to make sure it was as strong as it needed to be. He kept hold of the noose to prevent One-Thumb from getting away or just falling over.

Both of the other men had watched what transpired. Neither of them reached for the guns at their sides, but it was plain to see that they could arm themselves in the time it took to blink.

Before too long, Deke let go of the younger man's hand. Nodding once, he said, "This is a job like any other, Wilde. You should conduct yourself like a professional or you'll never be taken into account."

Hearing himself addressed the way he preferred took some of the edge off of the younger fellow. Born Spencer Wilde, he learned at an early age to appreciate one name over the other when it came to playing the role of a man to be feared.

"All right, Deke," Wilde said. "I'll try to hold my tongue."

Shifting his dark, steely eyes toward One-Thumb, Deke added, "Besides, if it's death you want, you won't have to wait much longer."

Up to this point, One-Thumb was calming down a bit. It seemed as though he'd made peace with his predicament, but that went right out the window once he heard Deke say those words. "Aw, Jesus Christ. You're not still gonna do this, are ya?"

"Got no choice, One-Thumb," Deke said, stepping back to watch over the proceedings.

"You could let me go. I'd head wherever you want me to go and I wouldn't come back. Not ever! I swear!" Tears were starting to well up in the corners of One-Thumb's eyes and Wilde pounced on that sight like a coyote on a fresh kill.

"You can go to hell," Wilde hissed as he cinched the last knot wrapped around the thickest part of the tree stump. "How about that?"

Before Deke could step in again, the man who'd been working on the noose stepped back. "All done here."

The fourth man returned the glance that Deke gave him and nodded. "Here, too."

"Slip that rope off his neck," Deke said.

For a moment, One-Thumb looked as though he'd just gazed upon the golden face of the Almighty himself. When the man behind him removed the noose, he started to let out a relieved breath.

That breath stuck in his throat when he saw that rope get tossed over a thick branch and then brush against the top of his head after it came down again. From there, he didn't have time to do anything more than whimper before he was picked up by two of the men so Deke could secure the noose around his neck.

"Christ, Deke, you can't do this. You know I didn't do nothing wrong."

Deke looked up into One-Thumb's eyes as he tightened the noose. Even though he was taller than most men, he could just barely reach the knot to tighten it. He knew he didn't have to get it too tight; the weight of One-Thumb's body would cinch it tight enough to do the trick.

"It ain't my job to make that decision," Deke said plainly. "It's the judge's. You know that."

The rope chewed into One-Thumb's neck. Its dry, rough edge peeled away the top layers of skin once the men that were holding One-Thumb up even started to let go. Feeling the noose dig in a little deeper, One-Thumb struggled to straighten his back so he could take one last, gasping breath.

"You know he's wrong, Deke! That judge is—"

The rest of One-Thumb's words couldn't make it out of his mouth once the two men holding him suddenly let go. It was a short drop, but it was all that was needed. The branch strained with its new weight, but held just fine. The rope creaked as One-Thumb started to swing in the strong breeze. He swung even more once one of the men slapped something against his chest.

All the while, One-Thumb strained to finish what he'd been saying. It didn't matter that his neck was being forced shut by the rough grip of the noose. It didn't even matter that the men he'd been talking to were already turning their backs and walking away.

It was a short drop, but One-Thumb Ambrose would be falling for the rest of his life.

TWO

It had been a while since Clint Adams had been to Dodge City. After spending some time as far north as Canada and Wyoming in the last couple of months, he was looking forward to spending some time in a more familiar place. The north was fine for a while, but Clint had had his fill. The sight of mountains and snow had just started to look like rough terrain and frozen water to his weary eyes.

It felt good to be heading to such familiar stomping grounds. Of course, part of that upswing could be chalked up to the change of the seasons. After a particularly grueling winter, spring was on its way. And unlike those days when it only felt as though warmer days were coming, it was about time for those changes to stick.

Riding on the back of his Darley Arabian stallion, Eclipse, Clint pulled in a lungful of fresh air so he could savor it like a mouthful of wine. He was no connoisseur, but Clint knew what he liked and he liked the taste of springtime air just fine, indeed.

"What do you say, boy?" Clint said to the back of Eclipse's head. "You ready to ride the streets of Dodge again?" Even though he knew better than to expect an answer, talking to the horse still seemed like the most natural thing in the world. It was one of those things that just became acceptable after a while, much like talking to oneself.

Clint had been riding for a few weeks and still had another week to go. Passing through the southern part of central Nebraska, he could have made it to Dodge in less time if he pushed Eclipse to his limits, but Clint didn't want to strain the horse for no good reason. More than that, he was enjoying the leisurely ride toward Dodge. It gave him time to soak up and enjoy the simple pleasures that came along with riding just for the sake of riding.

He had no jobs to do or obligations to fulfill for a change. Rather than think about that for too long, however, Clint let his mind wander in another direction. It seemed that when he started enjoying his freedom too much, something always came along to take it away from him.

Clint Adams was a known man.

The reputation he lived with wasn't anything he'd asked for, but he would be lying if he said he hadn't earned it. More often than not, folks knew who he was either on sight or soon after. There were plenty of stories going around about him and the adventures that had filled his life. Most of those stories were a lot of hogwash.

On the other hand, it was during those exploits that Clint had gotten to be so handy with the Colt revolver that he'd modified himself. And the better he got with that pistol, the more exploits he could afford to get into, and with that, there came more stories about those same events.

It was a vicious circle that Clint had given up on trying to stop long ago. What it boiled down to was that he lived his life the way he wanted and helped out other folks whenever he could. All the rest wasn't his concern. People would say what they wanted whenever they wanted. There simply wasn't a thing to do about it.

Another thing that Clint had realized was that, no matter how much he said otherwise, he wasn't the type to sit still for very long. That didn't just cover the way he rode from one town to another as if the wind picked him up and carried him along. It meant that he thrived on the excitement of his life just as much as others thrived on talking about it.

He smirked and shook his head when he thought about that, knowing it was only too true. It would have been easy to find a good woman and pick a good spot to sink some roots. But that would deprive him of all those other pretty spots waiting for him out there, not to mention all the other good women.

One such woman was a sweet little saloon girl named Misty who lived in a little place called Trickle Creek. She was one of those girls who seemed to light up any room she entered, and yet she still chose to live in a town that was only known for a water source that was too stubborn to dry up.

Clint smiled when he thought about her. He wasn't sure how long it had been since he'd seen her, but he never really kept close track of those things since that was a good way for a man to feel old. What he knew for sure was that it had been too long since he'd seen her and that was enough to decide on Trickle Creek as his next destination.

It was as simple as that.

One decision based on a fond memory and Clint was on his way. That was the beauty of living free and riding fast. That was the reason Clint would never give up the life he'd fashioned for himself. With that decided, Clint looked around and took a quick survey of his heading. He was already headed south toward the Kansas border, which meant he wasn't too far from Trickle Creek.

Perhaps he'd already decided to go there and just didn't realize it. Sometimes, no matter how free he liked to think he was, Clint got the sneaking suspicion that there was something guiding him after all. If he was more of a spiritual man, he might consider it some mild sort of divine intervention that led him to where he was needed.

But Clint was more of a gambler, which put those sorts of things strictly under the heading of luck. Either way, he still liked to think that he was the one calling the shots. Life was just simpler that way. Besides, there wasn't much he could do about it no matter which answer turned out to be right.

"I definitely need to get to a town," Clint said to Eclipse. "No offense, but if I don't get someone else to talk to, I might just drive myself crazy."

And, just like that, the wheels of fortune turned.

No less than a few seconds passed before Clint was reminded of another parable: Beware what you wish for, because you just might get it.

Clint had asked for someone else to talk to and he spotted that someone as soon as he cleared the top of a rise and got a look at the flatlands stretched out in front of him. What caught his attention was a cluster of trees. Soon after that, he spotted the only other fellow he'd seen for a few days.

Unfortunately, since that other fellow was swinging by a rope from the biggest of those trees, he probably wouldn't be up for much conversation.

THREE

Clint snapped the reins and Eclipse answered the call without a moment's hesitation. The Darley Arabian brought Clint to those trees in no time at all. He swung down from the saddle even before the stallion came to a full stop and went over to get a closer look.

It wasn't the first dead man Clint had ever found. It wasn't even the first hanged man he'd found. But there was something that caught Clint's eye about this one. There was something stuck to the hanged man's chest and it appeared to have been tacked right into his skin.

Frowning as he got a closer look, Clint saw that the tacks had indeed been knocked right into the front of the body. There was just a little blood around the entry points, which were uneven and about an inch apart. The tacks held a piece of parchment onto the body as if that dead man's torso was just another empty section of wall.

Clint reached out to keep the body from swinging in the wind so he could read what had been scrawled onto the parchment. All it said was:

LAWBREAKER
HUNG FOR HIS MISDEEDS

BY THE ORDER OF
JUDGE H. KRUEGER

It wasn't much as far as epitaphs go, but it made its point well enough. The letters were written in a fluid script, and upon closer examination, Clint saw that the ink wasn't fully dried in a few spots. He was looking at that when suddenly the entire parchment rattled in his hands.

Clint wasn't easily scared, but having a dead man twitch was enough to give anyone a start. Taking a quick half step back, Clint reached for his gun out of reflex. He stopped himself before clearing leather. Something else had caught his interest. It was a sound that had been lost in the wind up until this point. Now that the wind had died a bit, Clint could hear the slight, scratchy rasp coming from the dead man swinging in front of him.

Stepping forward once again, Clint got closer to the body and steadied it with both hands. Sure enough, there was a sound coming from the hanged man and that was enough to spur Clint into immediate action.

The first thing he did was grab the body around the waist with both arms. From there, Clint lifted enough so that all of the man's weight wasn't tightening the rope around his neck.

"Hold on, mister," Clint said while strengthening his grip with one arm so he could free up the other. "Try to hold your breath and relax for just a few more seconds."

Clint could feel the man's chest expanding slightly. Although the fellow wasn't straining against him too much, it would have been impossible for him to relax given his current predicament. All the same, Clint did his best to hold up the awkward weight while reaching down to grab the knife from his boot.

There was a tense moment or two where Clint nearly lost his balance while lifting his leg to get to his knife.

Somehow, he managed to pull off the ungainly maneuver and the knife was soon in his grasp. The muscles in Clint's back and shoulders strained, not so much from the other man's weight, but from the odd angle from which he was trying to hold that weight.

"Here we go," Clint said, his own voice straining as he reached up to cut the rope over the top of the noose. "Just . . . hang in there."

For a moment, Clint thought the man was going into some sort of fit or convulsion. As he sawed the blade through the rope, however, he could tell the man in his grasp was actually laughing. It was a rough, haggard sound, but a laugh all the same.

The knife snapped through the rope after a few more digs and both men dropped to the ground. Clint twisted his body to the side to keep both of them from landing too hard or from landing on the knife. In the end, they wound up stretched out in the dirt and fighting to catch a breath.

Of course, the man with the noose still around his neck was fighting just a bit harder. Even so, his chest and shoulders were still shaking with laughter. The more breath he pulled into his lungs, the more boisterous that laughter got.

"That," the man with the noose wheezed, "has got to be . . . the worst choice . . . of words I've . . . ever heard."

If Clint had been in a better frame of mind, he might have caught the other man's meaning a little quicker. As it was, he had to think about it for a moment before recalling having told the man in the noose to hang in there only seconds ago. Now that he remembered, Clint couldn't help but smile a bit himself.

"Oh yeah," he said, feeling relieved that the other man was still healthy enough to breathe and even laugh. "I guess I'm a bit rusty on manners regarding talking to men I find hanging from trees."

The other fellow let out a gasp, touched his hand to his

neck and immediately lost his smile once his fingers found the noose that was still there. Both hands went to the rope and he winced when his fingers brushed against the tender skin beneath it.

"Damn, that burns," the man said in a raspy tone. "But I got to tell ya, it feels a whole lot better than swinging in this breeze."

"You should probably leave that rope there for a moment," Clint said. "At least until you catch your breath." Having said that, Clint took a moment to catch some breath for himself. All the while, he didn't take his eyes off the man he'd just cut down from that branch. "By the way," he said after a few more seconds, "I'm Clint Adams."

The man with the noose reached out to shake Clint's hand. Once his fingers closed, he said the very same two words that jumped into Clint's mind. "One-Thumb."

Clint could feel the absence of the important digit, but didn't make a big show of it.

"One-Thumb Ambrose. Actually, there used to be more to it, but it's just One-Thumb now." He held up his wounded hand and shrugged. "I guess that's true in more ways than one."

FOUR

"So how did you wind up swinging from that tree?" Clint asked. He'd waited a minute or two to ask the question, but there just wasn't a tactful way to go about it.

One-Thumb was fiddling with the noose again. Sitting against the tree that had almost been the death of him, he gathered his strength while taking deeper and deeper breaths. Even though the rope had been loosened, he still felt as if it was chewing through his flesh. Then again, he wasn't too wild on the notion of keeping the damn thing around his neck, either.

"How'd I wind up there?" One-Thumb repeated. "It wasn't no climbing accident, that's for damn sure."

Clint didn't respond to this joke the way he had to the first. This time, his eyes remained fixed and a smile didn't even start to come onto his face.

Once he saw that Clint wasn't going to be deterred, One-Thumb gritted his teeth and yanked the noose up over his head. The skin around his neck was red and gnarled. Blood trickled from spots here and there, but it wasn't enough for either man to fret over. One-Thumb tossed the noose toward his feet and brushed his fingertips against the bloody skin at his neck.

"Actually," One-Thumb said, "I was gonna ask why you cut me down."

"How about you answer my question first?"

"All right. I certainly owe you that much. I was strung up there for horse thievin'."

"Whose horse did you steal?"

"I didn't steal no horse. I borrowed it."

Clint laughed and rubbed his hands on his eyes. "That's real original. Let me guess. Judge Krueger didn't believe you."

One-Thumb laughed as well, but there wasn't a lick of humor in his tone. "Believe me? Hell, he barely even listened to me. That son of a . . ." Trailing off, he cocked his head and looked over at Clint once more. "Wait a minute. How'd you know the judge's name?"

Clint leaned down and reached out to tap his finger against the parchment still tacked to the man's chest.

Reflexively, One-Thumb grunted and started to pull the parchment off of him. As soon as he tugged against those tacks, he winced and let out a sharp, pained breath. "Ow, Christ! I forgot about those goddamn things." Reaching up to pluck the first tack from his skin, he said, "With everything else that was going on, I didn't really feel this at the time." He paused, sucked in a breath and pulled out the second. "I feel 'em now, though, that's for sure." He winced, paused and then finally took out the last tack. "I guess that's a good sign."

"Considering how I found you, the fact that you can feel anything at all is a real good sign," Clint said.

Nodding, One-Thumb looked down at the bloody tacks in his hand before tossing them over his shoulder. He then picked the parchment off his chest and looked it over. "Judge fucking Krueger. If I had to guess, I'd say he was the devil himself."

"You were the one who borrowed those horses."

One-Thumb looked disgusted as he glanced up at Clint.

"And if you're so convinced I'm an evil man, why'd you bother to cut me down from there?"

"First of all, I never said you were evil. I've just talked to more robbers than I can remember who look at every one of their crimes as a loan."

One-Thumb smirked slightly. "Yeah, I guess that does sound pretty weak."

"And secondly," Clint continued, "I don't look kindly on murder, no matter who's at the receiving end of it."

With his eyes flaring wide, One-Thumb climbed to his feet as quickly as he could manage. "I didn't murder nobody," he said sternly. "Not even that goddamn judge accused me of something like that. And I don't care how you helped me, I can't let you say—"

"I wasn't talking about you murdering anyone," Clint interrupted.

Although the anger was fading away from his expression, One-Thumb still looked confused. "Then what were you talking about?"

"I was talking about what happened to you. If I hadn't come along, you would have died and I see that as murder."

"Nobody said it like that before. They all just said I was being hung in accordance with the law."

Clint reached out and took the parchment from the man's hand. "You shouldn't believe everything you read. Legal hangings take place on a public gallows with legal witnesses present. This," he said, pointing up toward the rope dangling from the tree branch, "was a lynching. And I don't care how they get justified, lynchings are murders."

One-Thumb looked at Clint for a few moments. Those moments passed in silence until he brought his hand up to touch the rough flesh that had been scarred by the noose. "The only thing I could think of when I felt that rope around my neck was that I was gonna die. When I started to swing and choke with my feet so close to the ground, I prayed that I would just hurry up and die.

"Then, after a while, I figured dying was the best thing for me seeing as to how my life turned out. Now, I'm starting to think I wasn't meant to die after all. Maybe there's still something I can do with the time that I was given today."

"If you were meant to die, you'd be dead," Clint stated. "It's as simple as that. As far as doing something else with your life, I'd say you should definitely rule out the possibility of being a horse thief. You weren't too good at that."

One-Thumb started to look insulted, but his face quickly broke into a smile. "You got that right."

"Do you live around these parts?"

"Sure do. I live in Trickle Creek. It's only about—"

"I know where it is," Clint interrupted. "Come on. You can ride with me."

Clint was certain he could have saved himself a whole lot of grief if he'd just set One-Thumb on his way and been done with it. But there was more to be done than just putting a stop to a lynching. Not only did Clint just happen to find One-Thumb, but both men were headed for the same town.

Some things were just meant to be and Clint knew better than to fight it.

FIVE

Eclipse stomped through the namesake of the town directly in front of him just before passing the shacks marking its northern border. The creek was even smaller than Clint remembered and appeared to be more of a puddle that had been stretched out from one end of town to another. He'd seen bigger bodies of water formed after a moderate rainstorm and had heard louder splashes in bathtubs.

The town itself wasn't much more impressive. Although it had grown a bit since the last time Clint had seen it, Trickle Creek was still laid out the same. It branched out in both directions on either side of the little path of water, which somehow still had enough gumption to keep flowing. It was approaching dusk when he and One-Thumb arrived and the town was actually starting to show some signs of life.

From a distance, it had seemed all but deserted. Clint spotted the first cluster of buildings some time ago, but had to strain before he could pick out any shapes moving among them. Now, however, Clint could hear more voices starting to rise up over the sound of Eclipse's footsteps, as well as the sound of music drifting among the rattle of wagon wheels. Soon, Clint felt a tap on his back which caused him to bring Eclipse to a stop.

"That's a fine horse you got there," One-Thumb said as he swung down from the saddle. His voice was still rough, but that hadn't kept him from talking almost nonstop throughout the entire ride. "I sure appreciate you bringing me this far, but I can walk from here."

"You sure it's all right?" Clint asked. "I mean, there's still plenty of folks out there who won't be too glad to see you." Even as he said that, Clint heard some excitement brewing to his right.

One-Thumb glanced over in that direction as well. The moment he got a look at the source of the excitement, his smile returned. "I know you're right about that, but it looks like my luck's holding out one more time today."

Clint could see the commotion was being caused by a woman about twenty yards away. She was standing outside a small building and had been watching Clint since he rode into town. She didn't start getting loud until she could see the man sitting behind Clint.

The woman was heavyset and rounded in every way. She had large breasts that swung like pendulums as she walked in a fashion that was part stride and part waddle.

"Jeremiah Ambrose," the lady shouted. "Is that you?"

One-Thumb shrugged as though he could already feel his bones being crushed between the woman's thick arms. Looking up to Clint, he said, "That'd be my wife. I should probably go comfort her and tell her what happened."

Clint nodded quickly. "Yeah, you do that." He felt even more urgency once he saw that the large woman had gotten herself moving in his direction. She was smiling and seemed friendly enough, but came at Eclipse like a freight train that had built up some powerful momentum after rolling down a hill.

"Oh my lord, Jeremiah, it is you! It is you!" One-Thumb's wife hollered. She was only a few more paces away and there was nothing her husband could do but brace himself for impact.

"It's me, Delia, but try not to—"

The rest of One-Thumb's plea was squelched as the large woman's arms wrapped around him and squeezed with all the power she could muster. The smile on Delia's face was wide and her eyes closed as she wallowed in the moment. It wasn't until she opened her eyes again that she even realized she'd picked One-Thumb clean off his feet.

"I was so worried," she said. "I heard some things that were just terrible, but I'm so glad to see you home again." Setting him down while keeping him at arm's length, she took a more careful look at him. As soon as she got a better look, her eyes widened and the color drained from her face. "Oh . . . my . . . God! What happened to you?" she asked, while tears leaked from her eyes.

Squirming ineffectively in his wife's hands, One-Thumb was unable to get his arms free. "I'll tell you all about it, darlin'. But you're gonna have to let me go."

Ignoring what her husband had said, Delia turned her gaze toward Clint. "Who's this one? Did he hurt you?"

"Don't get too riled up, ma'am," Clint said while steering Eclipse back from the advancing woman. "I brought your husband back. I was just trying to help."

"He's right, Delia," One-Thumb cut in. "He saved my life."

That stopped the woman in her tracks. When she looked back to her husband, Delia returned to crying gratefully. "Oh, I'm so happy you're home. You wouldn't believe what I've been hearing all day long." She clasped him to her, nearly suffocating him by burying his face in her massive breasts. "They say you stole that horse your cousin lent to you!"

Suddenly, she reached up to Clint with both hands as if she meant to yank him right off Eclipse's back. Instead, Delia reached up to hug him around the waist as best she could while saying, "Bless you, mister. Jeremiah can be a trial and Lord only knows why I married him, but bless you for keeping him alive."

Clint bent in the saddle and did his best to return the hug. "I'll stay in touch, ma'am. And if you need to find me, I'll be at the Herd Water Saloon."

She looked strangely up at him, which prompted Clint to ask, "Is the Herd Water still here?"

"It is, but you're perfectly welcome at our place rather than staying there."

Clint glanced over to where One-Thumb was still being squashed within an inch of his life. "It looks like you could use some time alone. We can meet up once we all get some rest."

"Well take this before you go," Delia said, reaching into her more than generous cleavage with one hand. When she pulled her hand out again, she was holding a large cross that had been hanging from her neck by a silver chain.

"Oh, I couldn't," Clint said.

Delia was already pulling Clint down so she could loop the chain around his neck. "Nonsense. I insist."

Rather than get yanked out of his saddle, Clint accepted the cross and tucked it under his shirt. Delia smiled widely and gave some quick directions to their home. After that, Clint tipped his hat and rode away from the couple. The more time he spent with that wailing woman and her squirming husband, the more that gruesome tree with the rope hanging from it seemed downright peaceful.

SIX

The Herd Water Saloon was so named as a kind of slap in the face to the town itself. While the town founders had seen the pitiful little stream as something to be proud of, the owner of the saloon looked at it like most of the other locals, who said the creek looked more like the piss running off from where the cowboys kept their herd.

It wasn't a good name for a town, but a perfect one for a saloon. Especially for a saloon as loud and boisterous as the Herd Water. Clint could hear the place when he was three streets away, and that was impressive considering that the nightly rush had barely started. The sounds drifting down the street ranged from bawdy laughter to angelic singing. A piano player was adding to the mix, giving the air the feel of a strange dream.

Since he'd been looking forward to visiting that particular saloon, however, Clint appreciated every last bit of that noise. In fact, he quickened Eclipse's steps until he was close enough to be fully immersed in it. Like anyone else who'd spent their fair share of time in saloons, Clint quickly filtered out the sounds that were most common. In this case, it was the loud swearing and louder laughter. That left him with one sound in particular that called to him like a siren calling to doomed sailors.

Tying Eclipse to a post not too far from the Herd Water's front door, Clint smiled and soaked up that sound. He'd been remembering that singing for some time and had always figured that he'd been building it up in his mind. Now that he was close enough to hear it for real, however, he realized that he hadn't been doing it justice.

Although it was hard to discern the exact words being sung, Clint had no trouble picking up on the melody. That alone was worth the trip, as well as all the trouble along the way. In no time flat, he was at the front door, which was being propped open by a spittoon brimming with thick brown fluid. Clint stepped inside and immediately had to dodge an incoming fist which was aimed at the side of his head.

After all that had happened lately, Clint's reflexes were plenty sharp and he was able to easily duck under the blow. When he got a look at who'd thrown it, that fellow had already found his true target and was throwing himself headfirst in that direction.

The fight that ensued was a flurry of fists, elbows and boots. Almost as soon as it started, it was forced outside by a hulking mass of muscle wearing a bowler hat. The monstrous figure absorbed a few punches which he didn't even feel and tossed both fighters out by the scruffs of their necks.

Clint sidestepped that little scrap and waded even farther into the chaos within the saloon. The bar stretched along the left wall, and the right wall was taken up by a long, narrow stage. In between were tables set up for all sorts of gambling as well as a few that were just for holding drinks. The floor was wet with liquor and worse, but Clint had been in enough saloons to be able to compensate for the unsure footing.

Once he was away from the bar, it was easier to navigate through the bodies that were shifting every which way. The stench of cigar smoke mixed with whiskey tainted his nose, but his eyes and ears were already kept satisfied enough to make up for it.

There weren't any empty chairs near the stage, which was where Clint wanted to be. Not wanting to turn back after making it that far, he merely picked out a spot as close to the stage as he could get and stood there with his arms folded over his chest. The look on his face combined with his solid stance was enough to deter most of the trouble-seeking drunks that came his way. The more dangerous of that sort didn't want to be that far from the bar in the first place.

On the opposite side of the stage from where Clint was standing, a man sat at a piano and did his best to bang on the keys hard enough to be heard over the ruckus. All in all, he did a pretty good job of fighting against the noise while maintaining some semblance of a tune. Then again, a screeching cat wouldn't have been able to tarnish the sound of the blonde's voice who stood at the center of the stage.

Even though she wasn't the only woman on that stage, the blonde drew every single eye in the audience to her. She was taller than all the other girls, who formed a line on either side of her. The chorus wore short black dresses which showed off some very impressive legs. But all of those curves combined couldn't stack up to what the blonde had to offer.

The blonde's dress was made out of white silk that wrapped around her body from her shoulders down to her feet. There were sections cut from the material to give mouthwatering glimpses of her full breasts, as well as a slit running down the skirt's right side. As she walked slowly around the stage, her hips shifted perfectly beneath the tight material as the audience was given alternating glimpses of her muscular calf.

Her hair was the color of spun gold and hung straight down past her shoulders without the slightest hint of a curl or wave. The lighting of the room made the place look dingy or even dirty in places, but played against her hair like rays from the sun.

When she sang, she formed her words using full, ruby lips. Her eyes moved over the crowd slowly as if to individually entice every single person looking back at her. The smile on her lips only made her dark eyes seem more mischievous and that, combined with the sultry curves of her body, made for a hell of a combination.

For a moment, Clint found himself rooted to the spot. It wasn't the first time he'd seen the blond singer, but there was no way to prepare himself to handle the sight of her much better. She was like a cool drink of water on a parched throat. Sure, a man had tasted water before, but at that moment there was nothing better in the world.

As soon as her eyes met his, the blonde smiled even wider and lowered her voice to a softer, more sultry tone. Clint, like every other man in earshot, felt himself responding to the sound of her voice. For the life of him, though, he had no idea what she was singing.

That was the way she performed. No matter what song came out of her, she sang it as though the words were her way of caressing the listener's skin. Clint could have snapped himself out of the trance, but didn't bother. Instead, he let himself be carried through to the end and applauded right along with the rest of that section of the room.

Although they'd been behaving for the most part, now that the music was over the audience got back to their rowdy roots. Men started jumping to their feet and jostling each other to get closer to the stage. The blonde only fanned the flames when she winked at the crowd and bowed just low enough to give them a little better look at her cleavage.

A skinny man wearing a light gray suit rushed onto the

stage and shouted, "Ladies and gentlemen, let's hear one more round of applause for our very own Misty!"

The crowd not only applauded, but started hollering and whistling as well.

"And let's not forget the rest of these fine ladies up here performing for you all!"

But the crowd didn't even seem to realize the man in the suit was still speaking. They were too busy being whipped into a frenzy by the sight of Misty bowing, flanked by the chorus of other leggy singers.

"Don't you worry," the man in gray said. "They'll be back soon after wetting their whistles. I suggest you all do the same."

The crowd heard that well enough and started harassing the serving girls walking among the tables.

As the singers started filing off the stage, the blonde gave Clint another look and pointed at him. She then pointed to the only empty table nearby before waving once again and slinking off stage. Knowing he was hated and envied by every man in the place, Clint walked over to the table and took his seat.

SEVEN

Misty was walking up to Clint's table in less than a few minutes. Actually, she was only walking at first—once she got through the door leading backstage, she was running straight to him. Clint stood up and held his arms open to catch her as she practically leapt into his embrace.

"Clint Adams! I can't believe it's really you!" she said in a voice that was still something close to the one she used on stage. Tapping his chest and giving him that mischievous look, she added, "I was certain you were going to ride away and become nothing but a fond memory."

Clint smiled and said, "Well, it's good to know that I'm a fond memory. And why the hell wouldn't I come back to see you?"

"I don't know. Men like you roam where they please and seldom get to the same place twice. At least, that's what I heard."

"Sure. And not one bit of that is based on personal experience." Clint looked into her eyes and waited until Misty looked away and started to laugh. "That's what I thought. You always were the type of girl who favored men that were no good for her."

"So that would leave you out, Clint. As I recall, you were real good for me." Toward the end of that sentence, her voice lowered to a sultry purr as her fingers traced a line up and down the front of his chest.

Clint could feel the same shiver going through him that he'd felt the first time he and Misty had gotten together. No matter how many women he met up with over the years, every one of them was memorable for something. A select few had earned their own spot in Clint's memories.

"Damn, Misty, you haven't changed a bit," he said, wrapping his arms around her and savoring the way she melted against him. "Not even that stage name of yours."

Stepping back and shifting her hips as Clint took one more look at her, Misty shook her hair over her shoulders and finally sat down. "I've had it since the first time I sang a note in front of someone, so I might as well keep it. Besides that, folks are starting to remember me and recognize my name."

"I'm sure that's not all they remember," Clint said, pushing in her chair before sitting down himself.

"It sure isn't. At least it better not be, considering how much I paid to get dresses like these made for me. You know this was made special? There's a lady backstage who sews me into it."

"I've never been more envious for another person's job."

Smiling and leaning forward, Misty placed her elbows on the table, laced her fingers together and rested her chin on her knuckles. That way, her arms perfectly framed the sinfully generous view of her glistening breasts. "No need to get jealous, honey. The job of getting me out of this dress is yours for as long as you're in town."

Clint leaned across the table until his face was so close to hers that he could see nothing but her eyes. He lingered there for a moment before stretching out a bit more, until his lips touched against hers. Misty's mouth opened just enough to tease him with the tip of her tongue before the kiss was over.

"I missed you, Clint," she whispered.

"It's always nice to be missed."

She leaned back just in time for a server to set some drinks on the table. "You still a beer drinker?" she asked.

"Always and forever."

"Good, because that's what I ordered you." Misty picked up her own glass, which was filled with red wine, and lifted it in a quick, silent toast. After taking a sip, she licked her lips and asked, "So what brings you into these parts, Clint? I don't suppose it was just to hear me sing."

"I've had some business north of the border that eventually led me back down this way. As soon as I got close enough, I figured there was no excuse to pass up a chance to come here and see you."

"Well, that's just fine because I've been thinking about you."

"Really?"

She nodded, making even that simple gesture seem sexy. "There's something I need to do, but I'd rather not do it on my own."

Clint picked up on the change in her tone, which had shifted from playful and alluring to something more serious. "Are you in some kind of trouble?"

"No, no. Nothing like that, although there have been a few unpleasant things going on." When she said that, her eyes shifted over to the tables near the stage.

Although he tried to follow her gaze and could tell that she was looking toward someone specific, it was hard for Clint to nail down exactly who that was. Nearly every face in the vicinity was looking at Misty and all of them responded to her glance as if it had been directed at them. Still, there was no mistaking the expression in her eyes when she looked back at Clint.

"What is it?" he asked, reaching out to put his hand on hers. "You can tell me."

"I know I can, Clint. You're one of the few men who I feel like I can tell everything to. Even the ones that treat me proper aren't as solid as you. And every man, even the nice ones, is always out for something." She took a breath and shrugged. "But that's fine just so long as I know what's going on. There's not much a man can think that I don't know about."

"Yeah, I definitely remember that about you. Behind those pretty eyes, there's someone most folks should look out for. That's why I don't like seeing you look so nervous. I don't recall you being nervous about much of anything."

"Well, just because I can figure out what's going on inside a man's head doesn't mean I can always do something about it."

"Well, if you're hoping to get something new from me, I'm afraid you might be out of luck," Clint teased. "I look at you and am thinking plenty of the same things that any man would be thinking."

"Actually, you'd be surprised."

This time, it was Clint who shifted to a more serious tone when he said, "No. I wouldn't. What's the matter, Misty?"

"Well, to cut right to the middle of it, I need a man like you around right now. I need a bodyguard."

"A bodyguard? Why?"

"Because there's men like that around." With that, she nodded toward a section of tables by the stage.

This time, Clint didn't have any trouble spotting the one she was talking about.

EIGHT

The man Misty was talking about was easy to spot mainly because he was glaring at her like she was on the menu. Now that Clint had an idea of what to look for and a general notion of where, picking the fellow out was no problem whatsoever.

He appeared to be a smaller guy, but with a stocky frame. His head was shaved clean, but not very well. Either his hair was naturally scraggly, or he cut it himself with a Bowie knife. But it was the eyes that gave him away. Like most other troublemakers, his bad intentions were practically reflected in his eyes. Clint could spot those kind a mile away.

In fact, being able to do just that had saved his skin more than once.

"He's the one with the shaved head?" Clint asked just to be absolutely certain.

Apparently, there wasn't a thing wrong with his instincts, because Misty looked away from the bald man and nodded. "That's him all right. I get the chills just knowing he's in the same room."

"Has he tried to hurt you?"

"Not directly. Well, not yet anyway."

"What's he done?"

Misty thought for a moment and stopped herself the first couple of times she started to talk. Finally, she took another sip of her wine and said, "I don't know. It started out with him coming to see me after my shows. Nobody's allowed back in the girls' dressing rooms, but they can get back there if they slip enough money into the right hands.

"Some of these fellas think that just because we're up there on stage, we're no better than the whores that walk around here. Anyway, this one over there came up to me a few times, had flowers brought to my room, even sent me some cheap piece of tin that barely passed as a necklace.

"After that, he must've figured he'd bought some privileges with me because he started following me around. One night he started to try to put his hands on me and I told him to go fuck a knothole." Her eyes darkened a bit with that, but another sip of wine brightened her up again.

"What did he try to do to you?" Clint asked.

"He tried to do a whole lot. As far as what he actually did, it wasn't much. I kicked him in the balls and told him to go to hell."

"You don't mince words, that's for sure."

"I know! And after all that, he still didn't leave me alone. Now he follows from a distance like some kind of vulture." She paused and rubbed her arms as though she'd suddenly caught a draft. "He's not the type of man to just go away when asked. He hurts people. I know it."

"Did you try going to the law?"

Misty looked at him as though Clint had started talking Chinese. "The law? What are they going to do? They'd probably fine me for attacking him."

"Is the law crooked around here?"

"Not exactly. They just stick to their own."

Clint shook his head and took a deep pull from his beer. Even that didn't help clear up his head too much. "So is this fellow a lawman?"

"I don't know. Look, I sing my songs and enjoy my life here. I've never had cause to get mixed up with the law and I don't like listening to rumors or stories about gunfighters and killing. All I know is that man scares me and I know he's going to try something else that I might not be able to stop."

Reaching out with both hands, Clint took hold of Misty's hands and rubbed them comfortingly. "All right," he said softly. "Sorry for asking so many questions."

"It seems like you don't believe me and I've got no reason to lie to you."

"I know. It's just that I need to know whatever I can before getting mixed up with someone who might be dangerous."

The blonde was verging on tears, but she sniffled and wiped her eyes with the back of one hand before she was crying. "I hate women that get all teary eyed at the first sign of trouble, and here I go doing that very thing. Jesus, I hate feeling weak."

Clint moved one hand up so he could brush it gently against her chin. Once he had her eyes focused on him, he said, "You're anything but weak. You just had a fright, is all. I can see that plainly enough."

"So you'll help me?"

Clint took one more look over toward that short man's table. The fellow wasn't glaring at them right away, but his eyes would occasionally shift over in Clint and Misty's direction.

"Actually, I'm surprised you don't have more men like that following you around. That's the type of thing you might expect for being—"

"If you tell me I've got this coming for looking and dressing the way I do, I swear I will bloody your nose, Clint Adams."

Clint lifted his hands in surrender before explaining, "I was going to say you might expect getting more of that for being out in front of such a rough crowd every night. You've got eyes and ears that work, Misty. You can see these are some hard cases coming through here, and drunk ones to boot. Have you ever thought about singing somewhere better? I'm sure the money would be better as well."

The aggression left her face just as quickly as it had appeared. "Oh, I am going somewhere better! That's the whole point." She took a few breaths and fanned herself with her hands as her excitement rushed back to a peak. "Of course I'm sick of performing for these leering drunks, but the better places only look for headliners every so often. I found a much better place that just happened to be looking and I need you to escort me to my new job."

"Well, that's great. Where is it?"

"A town called Origin," she said with a beaming smile. "Only a day or so ride from here. I don't want to take the trip unaccompanied, even on a stagecoach. I just wouldn't feel safe and I sure as hell am not riding there alone."

"Sounds like you've got every angle covered. That's more like the Misty I remember."

"So you'll take me?"

"When do we leave?"

NINE

Lou Garner was a man who was used to getting his own way.

It hadn't always been like that, but ever since he'd taken on his new responsibilities, Lou's life had been shaping up for the better. Most people he met respected him. Those that didn't respect him feared him. And those who didn't fear him were too stupid to know any better, which was how they usually wound up facedown in the dirt somewhere.

Lou had had his eye on the dancers at the Herd Water Saloon for some time. Despite the place's shitty name, it boasted some of the best working girls in the area. The girls on stage weren't all willing to share their bed for a fee, but the one that had captivated Lou most of all had gone several steps beyond simply rejecting him.

Misty had humiliated him. In fact, Lou had seen her glancing over at him when she was talking to her friends. Somewhere along the line she would start smiling and laughing and Lou was certain she was laughing at him. He didn't know for certain what she was saying to those others, but a man in his position couldn't afford to have anyone talking about him when his back was turned.

Not anybody.

Especially not some dancing girl in a shit hole saloon.

The more Lou watched her, the more plans he made for when he finally got her to himself. He tried to keep himself under control, but he was sure she knew what he was thinking. All the pretty ones were like that. They knew because they'd spent their whole lives teasing men and driving them to the very same edge where Lou now found himself.

He'd gotten closer and closer to her every day, but this day had turned out to be different. This day, Misty sat down and talked with a stranger whose face Lou sure as hell didn't like. The other man carried himself like he knew how to use the fancy gun at his side. He even had the gall to turn around and stare at Lou as though he didn't even know who he was gawking at.

Perhaps the stranger didn't know who Lou was, but surely Misty knew and surely she was telling him. He knew they were talking about him. He could feel it. And when he thought about that, Lou felt his blood start to boil and his hands clench into tight fists.

Lou didn't like people talking about him.

Not any woman.

Not any stranger.

Not anybody.

For the moment, Lou kept his anger bottled up and bided his time. Misty and that stranger talked some more until she finally got up. She was smiling as always and grabbed him by the hand as if she was leading him to have a dance in the middle of the room. If that happened, Lou wasn't sure if he could contain himself.

She belonged to Lou Garner and she knew it. All this fighting wasn't getting them anywhere, but if a fight was what she wanted, then that was what she'd get.

Every so often, Lou felt a twinge of pain in his crotch to remind him of what that blonde had done to him. He could still hear her words rattling around inside his ears as if she was still looking down and screaming at him. Anyone else would have been beaten to death for talking to him like that, but not Misty.

Lou had other plans for her, and those memories of what she'd done would only make him more determined to carry them out. Thinking about what it would be like when he saw those plans through was enough to cool the fire inside of him for a bit.

She wouldn't be laughing when it was just him and her, alone in the dark. She wouldn't have any more funny stories or smart comments to make when there was nowhere to go and nobody left to save her. And by the time he was done showing her what a real man is, Lou doubted she'd want to go back to the way things were anyhow.

In the end, she would be glad he'd pursued her for so long. And if she wasn't, then at least Lou would be happy. Oh yes. Just starting to think about getting his hands on her made Lou very happy indeed.

Misty and the stranger left the saloon arm in arm. They were both smiling and laughing, which made Lou certain that they were making jokes about him every step of the way. He managed to keep himself seated until they left, but when he got up, Lou nearly overturned his table.

That stranger couldn't take her away from him. After all the work Lou had put into getting himself a piece of that blonde's sweet ass, he wasn't going to let anybody keep him from claiming what was his.

Not anybody.

TEN

Clint tried asking Misty what she was doing when she practically dragged him out of the saloon. He tried asking her where she was going, but all he got in return was sneaky little smiles and shakes of her head. Then again, Clint didn't exactly need to be able to read minds to know what was on hers.

Every so often when she would look at him, Misty licked her lips in a way that even she wasn't aware of. The flicker of her tongue along her mouth was more instinctual, like when a hungry animal finally closes in on its prey. Clint had seen that look before on her face, and sometimes still saw it in his more pleasant dreams.

Once they were outside, he stopped asking where she was taking him and just enjoyed the walk. Winter was almost a memory but had just enough teeth left to make the nighttime air feel like a cool bite on bare skin. The wind was just strong enough to let out a low howl as it gusted between the buildings and down the street.

The wind played with Misty's hair like a pair of invisible hands, causing it to flow out and into her face like a silky veil. There was just enough moonlight to lend an almost unearthly shimmer to the silk wrapped around her body.

Having left in a hurry, she didn't put on a coat or even a wrap to keep the evening's chill away. Clint watched her move ahead of him, tugging at his arm and turning back and forth to anxiously keep an eye on him while also watching where she was going. There were plenty of others watching her as well. The men's eyes bulged out and their smiles were almost wide enough to catch flies. Of course, that lasted right up until the women they were with gave them a swift smack to bring them back to earth.

Clint watched Misty reveling in the night as well as the attention she was getting. Some people truly did belong up where everyone could see them and Misty was undeniably one of them. Her face was naturally bright, but that inner light became a smoldering fire when she saw that Clint's eyes couldn't have been taken off of her by anything short of a miracle.

All it took was a few moments in the cool air for Misty's nipples to become erect underneath the thin layers of silk clinging to her figure. Clint felt like he was walking in the mountains due to the fact that his breath was short from constantly being taken away from him. Her hand wrapped around his was the warmest thing in the world at that moment, and the thought of getting more of her skin against him started to gnaw at him from the inside.

Clint waited until they turned a corner before planting his feet and tightening his grip around her hand. As soon as she was about to ask what he was doing, he did the next best thing and showed her. With a snap of his wrist, he pulled her to him and she came without the slightest bit of hesitation.

Smiling broadly, Misty allowed herself to rush toward him and didn't stop until she was pressed up against Clint's chest. She closed her eyes and leaned her head back slightly until she felt Clint's lips settle onto her mouth.

At that moment, the wind gusted slightly, making the heat from their bodies seem all the more intense. Clint's hand moved on her hip, bringing her close enough to feel the erection growing between his legs. It took every ounce of strength she had to pull away from him at that moment, but it was worth it to see the shocked look on Clint's face.

This time, she really did drag him behind her as she headed away from the street and down a nearby alley. The space between the two buildings formed a cramped corridor that wasn't much longer than ten feet or so. She stopped at the end of it, let go of his hand and leaned back against the wall.

Clint looked at her standing there, glistening like a mirage in the shadows. Her eyes caught some of the moonlight as well, and wisps of steam came from her mouth when she parted her lips. Kissing her was the only thing he could have done at that moment. Waiting one more second would have been like asking Clint to let one of his arms fall off.

That first kiss was slow and passionate. It was the payoff for all the smaller kisses they'd stolen every so often throughout the night. It felt good to take their time and allow their tongues to slip against each other's lips. Clint hadn't exactly forgotten how good Misty tasted; it was more that he was taken aback by getting reintroduced to that pleasure.

His hands were reacquainting themselves with her as well. As good as she looked wrapped in skintight silk, she felt even better. Each curve was an experience, and he was in no hurry to experience every inch just yet.

Misty was taking her own time with him as well. She squirmed against the wall, writhing just perfectly against his body to drive him crazy. When she could feel his excitement growing harder, she smiled a bit and rubbed against him some more.

Even though Clint was enjoying where he was, he started looking around for somewhere else to go. He must have looked one too many times, because he soon felt Misty's hand on his face to prevent him from turning away one more time.

"Am I boring you?" she said with half a pout.

"Far from it. But if I don't get you alone real soon, I'm going to burst."

Peeling herself away from the wall, Misty took Clint by the hand and led him farther into the alley. They emerged in a small courtyard that opened onto the backs of several smaller buildings. "I know a place not too far from here," she said. Before she could say anything else, however, she was stopped by the feel of strong hands taking hold of her and pushing her against the wall.

Clint wasn't too rough with her, but he was just rough enough to bring an excited smile to Misty's face when he pinned her against the wall. "Too late," he whispered. "I'm not about to wait one more second."

He could feel the excitement coming off of her like a heat wave. When she pulled in a breath, she smiled widely and trembled as his hands ran down her hips to start pulling up her skirt. "What are you doing, Clint Adams?"

"You said you wanted me to take you, so I'm taking you."

"Thank God," she moaned as his hand slid between her thighs.

ELEVEN

Misty lifted her leg through the slit in her dress and wrapped it around Clint's waist. She could feel his fingers moving under her skirt and leaned back to allow the pleasure that he gave her to wash over her. When she felt his fingers brush against the lips of her vagina, she gave in entirely to the moment and opened her legs as much as she could to accept him.

She was wearing thin panties, but they were more of an additional texture to enhance the soft, warm surfaces he was feeling at that moment. Every second that his hand lingered there, he could feel her getting wetter through the delicate material. A little slow exploration with his fingertips was enough for him to find the sensitive nub of her clitoris, and when he touched that with one finger, she let out a moan that could be heard echoing through the night.

Misty opened her eyes and her face took on the expression of a naughty girl who was afraid of getting caught. She looked toward both ends of the alley, but kept grinding her hips against his slowly circling hand.

There were sounds of movement all around. Some of the sounds were from the wind; others came from animals rustling about here and there. Still others were people walking on the streets nearby, and the sound of them only made the smile on Misty's face even wider.

Clint looked around and saw the occasional local passing by at the end of the alley. The shadows around the spot he'd found were so thick, however, that he and Misty might as well have been wrapped up in a huge, black blanket. Besides, the notion of being seen at that moment only made the moment all the more exciting. Judging by the look on Misty's face and the groans coming from the back of her throat, she was thinking the exact same thing.

If Clint needed any more incentive to keep going, he got it in the form of small, swift hands working to unbuckle his belt and open the front of his pants. Clint's holster dropped to the ground and soon his pants were being tugged down. Misty's hand reached inside to wrap around his erect cock and start massaging it in long, steady strokes.

Clint heard the tear of silk as he kept pulling her dress up farther toward her waist. The slit of the side was doing well enough at first, but didn't go up as high as he wanted. Instead, his anxious hands had torn the material in his haste to get inside of her.

"Oh God," Misty groaned, being careful not to be quite as loud as she'd been last time. "Get in me, Clint. I want you inside of me now."

Thanks to Misty's efforts, all Clint had to do was lift her leg a little higher and take half a step forward to get his hips close enough to oblige. The moment he felt the tip of his cock press against the warm wetness between her legs, Clint felt his breath catch in the back of his throat. Her fingers guided him in until his entire length slid into the embrace of her moist pussy.

Her hands locked behind his neck as Clint began pumping in and out of her. The moonlight spilled down from the sky, giving her a silvery, luminescent glow which made the moment even more like one of the best dreams he'd ever had.

Misty was always like that. Everything about her seemed just a little too good to be true. Her voice, her body, even the way she made love made it seem as if no person could be that good. That could be a blessing and a curse, but Clint had never found it to be anything but the former.

Misty wasn't too good to be true, but she was the best at what she loved to do. She loved to sing. She loved to attract attention and she loved to fuck.

Rather than wonder if he was dreaming or not, Clint simply reveled in the moment and let her work her magic. Of course, she wasn't the only one hitting all the right chords. Misty's eyes clenched shut when Clint shifted his hips a certain way. Picking up on that signal, Clint shifted every so often and moved his hands on her body the way he remembered she liked it. Those things kept her eyes shut, her back arched and her hips thrusting insistently as if to beg him for more.

People were still walking by, but Clint was way past trying to see if they were looking into the alley. The night air blew around them and now Clint had both of Misty's feet up off the ground. Her legs were wrapped tightly around his waist, and there was enough strength in her dancer's thighs to keep herself there without him having to hold her up.

Her eyes opened now, and for a while Clint and Misty simply watched each other while he pumped between her legs. Clint looked down every so often to watch the muscles in her abdomen and legs tense as he thrust inside of her.

Her bare skin looked flawless in the moonlight and the pale illumination played beautifully against the slick, blond hairs between her legs. Misty's pussy clenched around him at the same time that her hands clasped him a little tighter. When he looked up into her eyes again, Clint found that devilish smirk back in its place.

"You like that?" she purred while clenching her pussy tight one more time. "Tell me you like it."

"God," Clint breathed. "I love it."

"I didn't hear you."

Clint knew what she wanted and didn't have any qualms about giving it to her. "I love it," he repeated in a voice that was a bit louder than even she'd expected.

She smiled at the way his voice bounced off the walls, and tightened her legs around him as a reward. The extra reward came when she felt him pound into her, and when he buried himself all the way inside, she clenched her pussy tightly around him.

Clint stopped what he was doing and turned to look down toward the other end of the alley. Misty immediately spotted what he'd seen and loosened her legs so she could step down onto the ground once more. There was a couple walking by who had now stopped at the end of the alley. They looked in toward Clint and Misty, but squinted uncertainly into the darkness.

"Hello?" the old man asked. "Is anyone there?"

Clint let Misty start to walk deeper into the alley, but stopped her at the last moment. They were both tucked in the depths of shadow when he grabbed hold of her by the waist. She almost let out a surprised squeal, but kept from making a sound at the last moment.

"Hello?"

"Oh, for heaven's sake," the woman accompanying the man at the end of the alley said. "It was just the wind or someone shouting from one of those god-awful drinking halls."

Clint's hands moved along Misty's hips, turning her around slowly until she faced the wall. From there, his hands traveled up again, moving along the sides of her breasts and then raising her hands up to just over shoulder height.

The old man was still squinting into the alley when Clint pulled Misty's skirt up once again to display the smooth, succulent curve of her backside. She had to bite down on her lower lip to keep from making a sound as she felt Clint's body pressing against her bare buttocks.

"Come on, George," the old woman said. "I told you, there's nothing there."

The instant the couple moved on, Clint was settling in behind Misty. His cock slid between her legs and entered the wet embrace of her vagina from behind. Misty pressed her palms against the wall even harder as she turned around to look at Clint over her shoulder.

Once Clint looked into her eyes, he had about a second and a half to react to what he saw.

TWELVE

When Clint would think back on that moment later, he would always wonder if he would have seen the same thing if he'd been with any other woman in that alley. The truth of the matter was that he'd never known a woman who seemed to shine brighter than Misty in her prime.

She was in her prime that night; Clint could attest to that much for certain. And as for her shining, she was more captivating than any star. Her eyes held his attention so much, in fact, that the dark form reflected in them stood out to Clint at that moment like something blotting out the sun.

All he saw was the reflection of something moving in her eyes. He couldn't see details, but he could tell that whatever was moving was headed in his direction. That was enough to get Clint to look that way and see the figure charging toward them even before Misty saw him. Sure, her eyes were the ones that had held the reflection, but her attention was diverted for a very good reason.

"Get down," Clint said, even as he was pulling Misty close to him and lunging for the ground.

As soon as he felt her safely touch down against the earth, Clint rolled off of her and tugged his pants back up around his waist. By this time, the man who'd been coming at them was close enough to make his first move and was already lashing out with his left hand.

Even if Clint couldn't see details of the other man's face, he could most definitely see the glint of moonlight off bared steel as a blade came screaming toward him. Fortunately, he'd moved himself and Misty quickly enough to dodge the incoming blade with just a duck of his head.

The blade scraped against the wall where Clint and Misty had been standing, sending splinters and paint chips raining down on them both. Misty was too frightened to scream. She was more concerned with drawing herself into a protective ball and covering her face and neck with both arms.

While remaining close to the ground, Clint waited for the knife to pass over his head before sending a sharp left jab straight up into the other man's ribs. The punch was short and sweet, its impact accompanied by the welcome wet snap of bones breaking beneath Clint's knuckles.

"Aw, son of a bitch!" the man with the knife grunted.

From down on the ground, Misty peeked from between her hands and stared up at their attacker with wide eyes. "Lou? Is that you?"

Just hearing his name spoken by her was enough to make the man with the knife stop what he was doing and even draw back a step. The blade was still in his grip, but his arm slackened a bit as his eyes focused more on the blonde cowering on the ground.

"You . . . know my name," Lou stated.

Misty let out a short breath and shuffled backward away from both men. "Of course I know your name. You've been after me for long enough."

Clint winced when he heard her say that. He could tell that the man was literally crazy about Misty and that the entire fight might be ended early if she only used that to her advantage. But whether it was because she was stubborn or just rattled, she didn't seem to be headed in that direction. In any case, Clint used the time she'd bought for him to get his pants hiked back up and his belt buckled.

"I have been after you, Misty," Lou said as though he was gazing at her through a fog. For the moment, he didn't seem to have picked up on the sarcasm in her voice. "That's why I came here to make sure that this one here didn't bother you for much longer."

Clint straightened up and slowly reached down for his gun. In his mind, he begged for Misty to see the power she had in this situation. Judging by the look she gave him as well as the confident nod, she was plenty aware of the sway she held over Lou.

"He's not bothering me," Misty said, her words acting like a stiff jab to Clint's gut. "He's more of a man than you'll ever be, and if you knew what was good for you, you'd run out of here before he makes you eat that knife of yours."

There was a moment of tense silence where neither of the men seemed to know quite how to react to what they'd heard. Lou was still chewing on the insult like a piece of grizzle that wouldn't go down and Clint was hovering with his hand halfway to his Colt.

The moment hung in the air for another couple of seconds. Clint let it hang, knowing that any sudden moves on his part would only push the fight back into motion. Part of him was still an optimist, and it was that part that made him think there was still a chance that Lou would come to his senses and realize he had no reason to fight.

Of course, there was the other part of Clint that knew better than to give someone like Lou the benefit of the doubt. Men rarely thought straight, especially where women were concerned. It was this part of Clint's mind that was proven right when Lou let out a low snarl and threw himself at Clint with his knife cocked back and ready to strike.

Since going for his gun would have meant Clint would have had to turn his back on Lou, he put that option right out of his mind for the moment. Instead, he swung his body at the waist with both arms held up and out to catch the incoming man head-on.

Clint's right forearm knocked against Lou's extended knife hand to bat it to one side. Still twisting around, Clint followed up with his left hand, which slid up Lou's arm starting at the elbow so his fingers could lock around the other man's wrist. Using Lou's momentum instead of going against it, Clint diverted the blade to one side and tightened his grip around Lou's wrist in the process.

Clint kept hold of Lou's wrist as he twisted his torso back around until his shoulder blades bumped against Lou's back. From there, Clint drove his right elbow into Lou's kidney hard enough to turn Lou's next breath into a painful wheeze. But Clint knew that wouldn't be enough to put the man down. He'd seen the look in Lou's eyes and recognized the tenacity that came along with being driven by rage and jealousy.

Sure enough, Lou managed to pull his knife hand free by twisting his arm and entire body against Clint's grip. He didn't stop there and instead kept right on turning until the blade was once again whistling through the air toward Clint.

It was all Clint could do to jump back fast enough before that sharpened steel slammed into his chest. Even with his quickness, Clint still felt the bite of the blade as it scraped through his shirt and sliced a shallow groove across his chest.

Lou smiled like he could smell the freshly drawn blood. His arm was already cocking back for another swing as he advanced on where Clint was standing. Misty was shouting something at both of them, but Lou was too far gone to listen and Clint was too busy trying to keep away from that blade.

Clint stood with his feet apart for balance and his arms open so he could catch or swat away an incoming swing.

Lou tested him with a few strikes and Clint managed to get out of the way of them all. Eventually, Clint felt his boots bump up against something on the ground and stopped there because his back was now to the wall.

"Walk away," Clint said. "Misty won't even be in town much longer, so there's no point in doing this."

Lou looked heartbroken. "Is that true?"

Misty nodded. "My last show is tomorrow."

"You're not going anywhere," Lou said. Backing away from Clint, he flipped the knife so he was holding it by the blade and then cocked his arm back until his hand was close to his ear. "If I can't have you, ain't nobody going to get you."

Clint saw Lou start to throw the knife, but was too far away to get to him before the toss was made, and once again the sharpened steel whistled through the air.

THIRTEEN

Clint took a quick hop back so he could flatten himself completely against the wall. From there, he hooked the toe of his boot beneath his holster, which he'd almost stepped on moments ago and had been careful to keep behind him the entire time. One upward snap of his leg sent the holster into the air just high enough for Clint to snatch the Colt from its resting place.

By this time, Lou had just straightened his elbow and was releasing the knife. The blade got far enough to turn a half circle through the air before Clint could squeeze the trigger of his modified Colt. The gunshot roared through the alley and smoke spewed from the Colt's barrel.

Before she could get her hands up over her face again, Misty saw sparks fly from the knife and heard the sharp impact of lead against steel. She wanted to scream, but the sound caught in her throat. Instead, all she could get out was a frightened yelp while tucking herself into a tight ball on the ground.

The big knife was still spinning down toward Misty, and Clint managed to adjust his aim, pull his trigger and hit it one more time just to be certain she was safe. Although her entire body twitched at the sound of the bullet hissing nearby, the blade was knocked even farther off its course until it clanged against the entirely opposite wall.

Clint stood up and turned the Colt's smoking barrel toward Lou. If not for the rush of blood still pounding through his ears, Clint might have smiled at the slack-jawed expression on Lou's face.

"I know you've got a gun on you," Clint said. "Take it out from wherever you're hiding it using two fingers and make sure to do it real slow."

Lou's eyes shifted back and forth between Misty and Clint. The anger seemed to have burned itself out of him, leaving only desperation and something that wasn't quite sadness. "I didn't want to hurt her," he said in a trembling voice. "I just wanted to be with her."

"Well, you've got a hell of a way of showing it. Now, get that holdout gun of yours."

Some men preferred knives and some preferred guns. The quickest way to tell which was which was simply to wait and see what a man tried to use first. But just because one man preferred a knife didn't mean he forsook guns altogether. Clint knew that well enough, which was why he didn't ease up one bit until Lou finally reached under his jacket to pull out a Smith & Wesson revolver.

Clint could still see the desperation in Lou's eyes. In fact, it was the moment where Clint was the most concerned during the entire fight. It was almost as though he could hear what was going on inside of Lou's head. The words might not have been coming through exactly, but the intent was clear enough.

If Lou wanted to follow through on what he'd started, this was the absolute last opportunity he would get. There was only one more decision to be made, but it was a damn big one and it was entirely in Lou's trembling hands.

"Don't be stupid," Clint said. "Can you hear that? Someone's coming, and after all the shooting, I'd bet it all that one of them's wearing a badge. You can either spend tonight in a cell or a box. It's up to you."

Lou turned around and saw that Clint was right. There were indeed people coming into the alley. They were shouting into the shadows and stomping between the buildings, turning the night into a chaotic mix of motion and noise.

But Lou's eyes shifted back around to fix once more on Misty. He then looked to Clint, held out his pistol and let it drop to the ground.

"Now kick it toward me," Clint ordered.

Only after Lou sent the pistol skidding toward him did Clint allow himself to let go of the breath he'd been holding. He bent down to pick up the gun and then tucked it away beneath his own belt. While keeping his Colt aimed at Lou, Clint stepped over to where Misty was huddled.

"You all right?" he asked.

To Clint's surprise, Misty straightened up and got to her feet so quickly that it seemed she was attached to a spring. Her arms looped around Clint's neck and her lips pressed against his mouth.

"All right?" she said. "I'm a hell of a lot better than that!"

"What's going on here?" a man wearing a badge asked from behind a shotgun that was pointed at both Clint and Lou.

"I'll tell you what's going on," Misty offered, without loosening her grip around Clint. "I witnessed the whole thing."

Fortunately for Clint, the lawman seemed to be just as taken with Misty as every other man with a pulse.

FOURTEEN

It turned out that the only thing better than a happy Misty was a grateful Misty. Clint spent the rest of the night in her hotel suite overlooking what passed for Trickle Creek's main street. She was so anxious to get him into bed that she practically shoved him over the footboard and tore the clothes from his body.

The upshot of that was that she then allowed him to tear the ruined silk dress off of her. The material split effortlessly, allowing her natural curves to be revealed. Clint's eyes were wide and he actually felt his heart slam in his chest.

"Kind of like Christmas morning, huh?" she asked while crawling on top of him.

Clint laughed, leaned back and savored the feel of Misty's body settling on top of him, enveloping him. "It'd take one hell of a Christmas to top this feeling."

She rode him for hours, satisfying his every need as well as a few others he didn't even know about. When she started to tire out, Clint rolled on top of her and took over until even he was too tired to do anything more than fall asleep.

He was awakened by one of the best dreams of his life.

When he opened his eyes and felt the sun warming his skin
through the window, he realized that he wasn't dreaming at
all. Misty's head really was between his legs and she really
was sucking on his cock as though it was the sweetest
candy she'd ever had.

"All right," Clint said while arching his back and running his fingers through Misty's fine, blond hair. "Maybe
we can get a late start after all."

After a hearty breakfast and a fresh change of clothes,
Clint left Misty's hotel and walked to the offices of Trickle
Creek's lawman. Even after he got there, he wasn't entirely
sure of the man's title. The only thing marking the building
was a painting of the badge that had been pinned to the
chest of the man in the alley from the night before. Shrugging, Clint entered the office and decided things would sort
themselves out soon enough.

"Good morning," Clint said to the familiar man sitting
behind a desk.

Looking at him with weary, hooded eyes, the lawman
obviously hadn't had a fraction of the rest that Clint had
enjoyed. "Mornin'," he replied.

The office resembled that of any lawman, complete
with gun rack on one wall and cells toward the back of the
building. Apparently there was at least one prisoner enjoying the hospitality of the town's jail because Clint could
see a pair of arms hanging out from one of the sets of iron
bars.

"Something I can do for you?" the lawman asked.

"Just checking in to see if everything's squared away
after last night."

"Sure enough." Getting up from his chair, the lawman
hooked his thumbs through his belt and sauntered over
toward Clint. "Believe it or not, I've actually handled a
fight or two in my day."

Without Misty in sight, the lawman obviously had no

reason to show even the first hint of respect toward Clint. The only thing on Clint's mind now was what had brought on the change in tension.

"No offense meant," Clint said lightly. "I've been in a few scraps myself and I know that—"

"I'm sure you know all about scraps, Mr. Adams, seeing as how you get into them on a regular basis. But this town isn't the type you're used to and we don't appreciate blood staining our streets. This isn't Dodge," the lawman said, stopping so that he was practically toe to toe with Clint. "And nobody here wants it to become like that place."

"Pity. Dodge has some fine theaters."

For a moment, the lawman didn't quite know how to take that. Finally, the subtle smirk on Clint's face came through, and the lawman backed off a bit. Not a lot, but a bit.

"Everything's handled, Mr. Adams. I'd ask for your gun, just to be safe, but I'm sure you probably won't be staying in town." That last sentence was unmistakably a statement of fact rather than any sort of guess or query.

"Actually, I will be moving on soon." Nodding toward the cells, Clint asked, "is that the fellow that was giving Misty all that trouble?"

The lawman's eyes narrowed and his mouth clenched as though he'd just bitten into a piece of rotten meat. "Why? You want to finish him off to impress that singer?"

"No. Just asking." When he saw that the lawman wasn't about to budge from his spot, Clint started to walk around the man so he could get to the cells. The lawman blocked him with a quick sidestep and placed his left hand flat against Clint's chest.

"You got no business back there," the lawman warned.

Clint looked into his eyes and then toward the cells. "That's not him, is it?"

This time, the lawman's scowl took on a different tone. This time, there was a bit of shame mixed into that expression. "No. It ain't."

"Where is he?"

"And why would that be your concern?"

"Because he tried to kill me and that singer, that's why. I'd like to know if he's locked up or if I need to do your job and make sure someone in this town gets the protections they need."

"He won't be bothering anyone in town. He's long gone by now."

Clint studied the lawman's face as he spoke. Using the same skills that served him so well at the poker table, he could tell the lawman wasn't exactly proud of what he was saying, but wasn't exactly covering it up either. "Why'd you set him loose?"

"Don't worry about that. I'm doing my job, and if you don't believe me, then you can go to hell for all I care."

"I guess that's fair enough, since this town's about to be short one singer anyhow." Turning toward the door, Clint started to leave but stopped and spun back around on the balls of his feet. "Oh, I almost forgot," he said once he'd caught the lawman's eye again. "Did you know that someone else in this town was almost killed?"

"Yeah? Who's that?"

"Fellow who goes by the name One-Thumb. He lives on the edge of town."

The lawman's eyes widened for a heartbeat and then narrowed again suspiciously. This time, however, there was no mistaking the venom shot through his stare. "What do you know about him?"

"Just that he was being lynched not too far from here. I thought as the town law, you might want to know about it."

The lawman's breath came in a forced wheeze, almost as though his lungs were being gripped by powerful hands. When he finally exhaled, he nodded and turned his eyes away from Clint. "I knew about it."

"Is there a problem with vigilantes around here?"

"You could call it that."

"Well, then I guess you've got everything well in hand," Clint said, not believing a word of it. "You might want to look after One-Thumb. Vigilantes don't take too kindly to people that disagree with their judgments."

"I'll look in on him, don't you worry."

With that, there wasn't much else to say. So Clint left the lawman's office, after sneaking in one quick glance toward the back of the room. As expected, the only prisoner there wasn't the man who'd attacked him and Misty the night before. Still, Clint knew it would have driven him crazy if he hadn't at least gotten a look for himself.

When he stepped outside, Misty was waiting for him and quickly fell into step beside Clint as he started walking toward the livery.

"Did everything go all right?" she asked.

"Not perfectly, but well enough I guess."

She shrugged her shoulders, which were bared thanks to the dress she wore. It hung down off both shoulders and drooped slightly in the middle to give just a mouthwatering glimpse of cleavage. Her skin seemed lightly tanned in the bright glare of the sun and her breasts bounced perfectly as she struggled to match Clint's pace. Even though she was dressed for a ride, she was still the center of attention.

"Well, Harvey Ambrose never was much of one for manners."

"Harvey? Is that the lawman's name?"

She nodded.

"I didn't even know you knew it," he said.

"I don't call him that. It just encourages him."

"Wait a minute," Clint said, stopping in his tracks. "Harvey Ambrose? As in One-Thumb Ambrose?"

She nodded. "Of course. They're brothers."

FIFTEEN

"What do you mean he got away?"

The words sounded less like a question and more like thunder rolling in from an approaching storm. The man on the receiving end of those words cringed reflexively and then immediately seemed to resent the fact that he couldn't help his reaction.

"Just like I said," Lou Garner explained to the tall, imposing figure who'd asked the question. "I checked in on him where we left him and this was all that was left." With that, he tossed the severed rope he'd been holding in his left hand. The coils hit the floor, exposing the noose that had been bundled up in the middle of them.

Deke Gray looked down at the rope as if it was a snake that had poisoned his mother. Every bit of that hatred remained in his eyes when he slowly shifted them upward to fix his gaze upon Lou. "You were supposed to stay and make sure he died."

"I did stay. It was just—"

Lou stopped what he was saying as Deke stepped up even closer to him. Deke was so close, in fact, that the sound of his breathing became like the churning of bellows beneath the man's chest. His nostrils flared and the whis-

61

kers of his thick mustache wavered only when he pulled
his lips apart to speak.

"Just what?" Deke asked. "What were you going to
say?"

"I . . . I . . ."

"Why don't I save you the trouble?" Deke said before
Lou could stammer one more syllable. "You were in that
saloon making eyes at that blond singer, weren't you?"

"It wasn't—"

"And don't lie to me, Lou. I'll know when you're lying
and I sure as hell won't appreciate it."

Lou's eyes had been straining to appear defiant, but wavered the moment his bluff was called. "I was there," he
said. "But so what? Ain't I allowed to go into town?"

"You can go into town as soon as your work is done. Jesus, any cowhand knows that. What the hell is wrong with
you?"

"That prick was swinging when we left him and—"

"And you were supposed to make sure he was still
swinging later that night." Deke pulled in a breath and
backed off a step from Lou. Only then did Lou dare to
move away himself. Until that moment, his feet might as
well have been nailed to the floor.

"How long did you stay there?" Deke asked, his voice
returning to a somewhat more normal level and tone.

Shrugging, Lou replied, "I don't know, I guess about—"

"Don't guess!" Deke roared. This time, his voice shook
the floorboards both men were standing on and was powerful enough to make Lou cringe like a scolded dog. "I want
you to tell me how long you were in town and don't try to
pull anything over on me."

"I was there most of the night. I found the cut ropes before dawn when I was headed out of town."

"There, now. Was that so difficult?"

"No."

"Did that asshole sheriff give you any trouble?"

"Him?" Lou asked with a short, snorting laugh. "He's too scared to do much of anything. I had to do most of the work to make it look like he was really taking me in."

Deke mulled that over for a few moments before finally nodding. "Good. That's real good." Looking over Lou's face, Deke scowled as if it was the first time he'd even noticed the bruises and red marks on the man's skin. "Looks like you got yourself knocked around a bit."

"It's not that bad."

"Still messing with that singer?" Deke didn't need a spoken reply to that question. The guilty look on Lou's face was more than enough to answer him. "I told you not to mess with them kind. You need to get yourself a woman who can cook instead of the ones that paint their faces up and parade in front of every man in creation."

"She's not a whore."

"I never said she was. She is trouble, though, and you'd be lying if you told me any different."

Lou turned away as his most recent memories of Misty floated through his mind.

"You'd best straighten yourself out," Deke said, suddenly draping his arm over Lou's shoulder like a concerned brother. "Tomorrow we see Judge Krueger, and I sure as hell won't be the one explaining this to him."

"You think he'll be mad?"

"No. He might have me kill you, but he won't get mad about it. This is all just business. But don't fret too much. I'd say he'll be more likely to set his sights on whoever cut ol' One-Thumb down from that tree."

Lou thought about that as well as what had happened to the last man who'd disregarded one of those warnings left on the chest of a hanged man. The recollection made Lou shudder and brought a wicked sneer to his face at the same time.

SIXTEEN

Misty had already arranged to rent a small carriage to take her to Origin. It was actually just a small cart that was pulled easily enough by a single horse, but she drove it like she was royalty on her way to her castle. Misty sat bolt upright in the driver's seat and snapped the reins to get the old nag moving. In the cart behind her, there was a pile of trunks and bags that nearly brought the cart down to its axles.

Clint rode Eclipse beside her. The Darley Arabian stallion even seemed to pick his hooves up in a trot to impress the blonde, who looked over at him approvingly.

"That's a fine horse," she said, smiling to Eclipse. "I think it likes me."

"He's a male," Clint replied with a shrug. "I doubt he's got much choice."

Misty took the joke as solemn fact and smiled widely. As if to prove that there was plenty of truth to what Clint had said, she got Eclipse to shake his head at her without much trouble at all.

"He does like me. Too bad Delia couldn't be here. She'd love to see a horse as fine as that."

Clint nodded at the mention of One-Thumb's wife.

Truth be told, he was thinking about Ambrose before she'd brought up the matter. He thought about what could have gotten One-Thumb hung from that tree and where he could have gone in the meantime.

Before leaving town, Clint had checked in on One-Thumb to make sure the man was all right. He knew the house was deserted when he first laid eyes on it, and a quick inspection of the place quickly confirmed that suspicion. The place was a mess, but it was the kind of mess left by someone who'd packed up in a hurry. There were clothes and belongings scattered about, but nothing vital.

Everything that could be used on the run was gone.

And One-Thumb and anyone else living in that house were also gone.

Considering what had happened, as well as what was bound to happen in the near future, Clint figured that was for the best.

"Where do you think they went?" Misty asked, as if listening in to what Clint was thinking.

"I honestly don't know. Wherever it is, I just hope it's far from here."

"You think his brother knows?"

"Probably. If he has any sense, he'll be keeping that bit of information to himself."

Misty shuddered and snapped the reins to keep her rented nag up alongside Eclipse. "Well, I can tell you one thing for certain. There won't be this kind of thing happening in Origin."

"Really?"

She nodded without the slightest shadow of a doubt. "Origin's almost as big as Dodge and all the famous acts come through there. They have real law, stores with Paris fashions and even an art gallery."

"Very cosmopolitan," Clint said.

"Of course. Why else would I be going there?"

Clint was about to suggest a few reasons that had to do

with offers of money or escaping the attentions of murder-
ous admirers, but decided against it. Actually, considering
the mood that Misty was in, he doubted that anything he
could say would even get through to her.

Suddenly, another thought entered Clint's mind. "Would
you say that Origin is the biggest town in the area?"

"Easily. There's a few that are close, but nothing com-
pares to the culture and prestige that Origin has been getting lately."

"What about a courthouse?" he asked.

Misty had to think for a moment, but then shrugged and
looked as though Clint was sprouting horns. "I guess they
have a courthouse." Just then, her eyes widened and she
perked right back up again. "I know they have one. The
theater isn't too far from it. There's also a shop close by
where you can buy dresses handmade by a woman from
Germany!"

"How big is the courthouse?"

Misty blinked a few times, as though she'd completely
forgotten Clint's original question. She then nodded quickly,
but the spark in her eyes faded away again fast. "I don't
know. Bigger than the dress shop."

"Bigger than your theater?"

"Hmmm . . . not quite. But it's close."

Clint nodded to himself. Most bigger towns had their
own courthouse, but not all of them had judges that
presided there regularly. It was common for judges to settle
in one area and travel around to the smaller towns as
needed. Sometimes judges were constantly traveling, on a
regular circuit.

More renowned judges, on the other hand, usually
stayed put. Considering the way the judge's name was
mentioned on the note tacked to One-Thumb's chest, this
Judge Krueger would seem to be fairly well known in the
area. If he was well known, he would probably hold court
in one place most of the time, and that place would be a

courthouse that was more of a permanent fixture, instead of the smaller buildings used on a circuit.

All of this went through Clint's mind in a matter of seconds. When he focused back in on what he was doing, Misty was in the middle of one of her own meandering trains of thought.

". . . but that dress shop doesn't have as many of the more elite fashions, of course, so I always try to stay in the smaller boutiques. They call dress shops boutiques in Paris. Isn't that wonderful?"

"Yep," Clint replied, knowing full well that she wouldn't have even noticed if he'd nodded off altogether.

The rest of the day was spent riding at a good pace, with Misty talking at triple the speed. Clint thought he could just let her talk as much as she wanted so she would hopefully burn herself out before too long. But without any interruptions, Misty only gathered that much more momentum.

The smile on her face as she described fashions, her singing and the theater she was bound for was positively beaming. A few hours of prattling on without end, however, took the sheen off of her bright, cheery face.

Clint found it helpful to just nod and mimic her reaction to what she was saying when he gave a simple, one-syllable reaction to it. That way, she would just go right on ahead and allow him to let his own mind wander. Once he'd perfected that technique, Clint actually found some peace of mind for himself.

The Nebraska prairie stretched out for miles in every direction like a sea of tall, waving grass and stalks of planted corn. Every so often, the terrain would get a little rocky or a set of hills would rise up beneath them, but it wasn't enough to present a challenge to the horses that were doing all the walking. In fact, Eclipse and the nag pulling the cart seemed to have picked up Clint's trick as well and were staring blankly ahead while moving their feet at a steady, mechanical pace.

When the sun began dropping toward the western horizon, Clint brought the horses to a halt. "Stay right here," he told Misty. "I'll go scout for a good place to make camp."

Misty's eyes widened and she glanced nervously about. "What? Camp? Here?"

"Well, we can't make it to Origin in one day."

"I thought we'd spend the night in a hotel."

Laughing under his breath, Clint held his arms out and motioned to the expanse of open prairie surrounding them. "I sure don't see any towns around here. Do you?"

"No."

"Then just sit tight and I'll pick out a spot."

Misty kicked the brake handle beside her, placed her hands on her lap and kept looking around, as if expecting to see a hotel sprout up from the dirt. That was just fine with Clint. At least she was quiet.

SEVENTEEN

The next morning, Clint was the one who woke up early and crawled over to slide up next to Misty. The air was crisp, clean and cold, and smelled like a mixture of all the wildflowers and trees around them. Clint had picked a good spot in a clearing not too far from a small cluster of trees which overlooked a wide expanse of open land to the south. When the sun rose, its rays sliced through the branches and warmed his face.

Misty was wrapped up in his bedroll and laying on her side. The evening before had been a rough one, with her complaining most of the time about everything, ranging from the weather to the bugs on the ground. She seemed to have calmed down a bit once Clint cooked dinner, and had gone to sleep after only a few more pouts.

As Clint moved up beside the blonde, he ran his fingers through her silky hair. The sunlight made it seem even more like spun gold. Her skin was warm and smooth to the touch, and when she felt his fingers upon her, Misty squirmed a bit as she shifted to turn in his direction.

"What do you think you're doing?" she asked in a tone that was frostier than the morning air.

Clint smirked and let his hand wander along the curve

of her hip. "Don't you like the fresh air?" he asked. "Doesn't the sun feel good on your—"

"The sun is burning my shoulder," she griped. "And there are still bugs crawling all over the bottom of this blanket of yours."

"That blanket's just fine. It's better than the one I used last night. That one usually goes over Eclipse when it's too—"

"Which is exactly why I don't want you to touch me," Misty interrupted. Jerking herself up and getting to her feet, she brushed frantically at the dirt, grass and stray leaves that clung to her dress. "I think some of those bugs got on me last night," she whined.

Realizing that he was in for a hell of a long day without any reprieve, Clint got up and helped dust her off. "There's not any bugs this time of year." Seeing the expression on her face, Clint corrected himself immediately. "I meant to say there's not many bugs."

"Well, however many there are, I can feel them on me! I would have liked to take a bath, but there's not even any water nearby."

The thought of Misty in a lake brought a nervous twitch to Clint's eye. "If you didn't like sleeping on the ground, then you sure don't want to wash off in a lake."

She let out an exasperated sigh and started scratching at a little dirty spot on her skirt. "Are we getting to Origin today, or do we have to sleep outside again like a couple of savages?"

"Believe me, we'll get there today. In fact, if we pick up our pace, I bet we can make it there even quicker than we planned."

"That sounds good. When's breakfast?"

Rolling his eyes, Clint wondered what had happened to the excited, energetic woman who'd been with him at the beginning of this ride. Rather than give Misty any more ammunition, he went over to his saddlebags and gathered up the supplies to cook breakfast.

The meal was quick and barely warm. At this point, Clint knew she would complain no matter what, so he didn't feel compelled to try to impress her with his cooking. Instead, they had coffee, bacon and beans before saddling up and moving out.

"You ready?" he asked, looking over his shoulder at Misty driving the wagon. Without waiting for a reply, Clint flicked Eclipse's reins and got the stallion moving at a slow gallop.

Behind him, he could hear Misty snapping her own reins and then the clatter of the cart's wheels soon followed. From there, the rest of the day was more than enough to make up for the rocky beginning. With Misty too busy trying to keep her rented horse in line, she wasn't in the mood for chatter. By Clint and Eclipse's standards, the ride was just brisk enough to break the monotony and actually made the hours slip by pretty well.

The sigh of relief Misty let out when she caught the first sight of Origin was loud enough for Clint to hear from his position up ahead of the wagon. He glanced back and found her still wrangling with the reins and struggling to maintain her posture while driving the cart. Although he slowed Eclipse down a bit, it wasn't by much.

Before too long, Clint and Misty were crossing over the town's limits and steering onto one of the streets that headed into the center of Origin. Judging by the smile on Misty's face, she could have been dragged there from the back of her cart and still would have been bright-eyed and bushy tailed.

"Oh, Clint, isn't it wonderful?" she proclaimed.

Clint took in the sights and sounds with a casual nod. "It's not bad at all."

"Just wait until you see my theater. You'll be knocked right out of your saddle."

Following Misty's lead, Clint came to a stop in front of a large, ornate building with a row of columns lining the main entrance. The building was so new that the air smelled like freshly cut lumber. It took up almost half a block and was two floors high. Long, flat steps worked a winding path up to the front door, giving the effect that the entrance was at least twice as high off the ground as it truly was.

All in all, Clint found the place to be a bit over the top. Misty, on the other hand, couldn't fawn over it enough. She jumped down from the wagon and started running as if she was being carried by a fleet of servants. Her steps became so bouncy and excited that she practically danced up the stairs and to the front door. When she got there, a squat, rat-faced man in his forties wearing a monocle was there to greet her.

"Welcome to the Neapolitan Theater," the man announced.

Clint waved to Misty and started putting some distance between himself and the theater before he was swept up into a drawn-out tour of the place. "I'll catch up to you later," he said.

But Misty wasn't even close to listening to him, which only granted Clint an even quicker getaway.

EIGHTEEN

After he'd delivered Misty safely to her destination, Clint's obligation for the moment was done. He meant to keep an eye on her, but another matter still pressed at him from another angle. That matter concerned a certain man he'd found swinging from the end of a lynch mob's noose, as well as a note cruelly tacked to that same man's chest.

The very thought of that made Clint grit his teeth. Lynching a man was bad enough. Tacking a note straight into his chest was adding one more sadistic insult to an already grievous injury. Clint didn't need to see the note to recall every line. The sight of it was still etched deeply into his mind.

Eclipse moved easily between the people walking or riding down the street in every direction. Wagons rolled by to add to the traffic, making the center of Origin seem more like a heart pumping blood through every available vein.

As he crossed the street and navigated through the people, animals and vehicles crossing his path, Clint had his eye set on one thing and one thing only. That thing was a building that was equally, if not more, impressive than the Neapolitan Theater.

Marked with a simple sign etched in gray stone, the courthouse stood in its place as though it alone pumped all the blood through Origin. The building was made out of brick and looked solid enough to have been standing there since the beginning of time. Stone, perfectly uniform, steps led up from the boardwalk and to the row of doors leading into the front of the building. Huge, sculpted lions guarded the entrance, glaring down at innocent and guilty alike with equal ferocity.

The building was impressive not only because of its architecture, but because of the power inherent within its walls. From the solid rock foundations to the hulking lions, and right down to the looming doorways, which were twice the size of most men, the courthouse was imposing. The sight of it hit upon every man's reflex to look away from something mightier than himself. Every time the doors slammed shut, a cringe could be seen on all nearby faces.

Clint dropped down from his saddle and tied Eclipse off to one of the long rails in front of the courthouse. From there, he walked the long path up to the front of the building. Along the way, he couldn't help but feel like a condemned man making his last walk toward the gallows. Now, more than at any other time, Clint could appreciate the resigned, defeated look etched across the faces of those about to hang.

Almost as soon as that feeling seeped into him, Clint wiped it out of his system. Replacing that sense of being overpowered was a feeling of resentment. Rather than be pushed down by the weight of authority forced onto him, he stared up defiantly at the courthouse and remembered the sight of poor One-Thumb Ambrose hanging from that tree.

It wasn't the most resounding of victories, but it was enough to make Clint feel better as he approached the building. Many judges tended to take on a sense of entitlement as soon as they donned their robes. Clint had seen enough trials to recognize the lofty way a judge might sit at his bench. Hell, even the job's title implied a whole lot, but that didn't mean that every judge let it go to his head.

Plenty of judges were good men trying to do their jobs and see justice carried out. But, just like in any profession with power, there were the bad apples that tended to mar the good name of the rest. Unfortunately, few people had the unique kind of power judges were given. One bad apple in that pile could put a seriously bad taste in a whole lot of mouths.

Clint was at the top of the steps, and stopped before entering the courthouse. He slipped his hand into his pocket and felt for something that had been driving him this entire time. His fingers brushed against the familiar texture, which was enough to spur him onward.

There were plenty of other people walking up and down those steps. Some of them were in military uniforms or wearing badges, while others were in the plain garb of workingmen. They moved alone or in groups. Every so often, one of the people passing by was in shackles and being led by armed officers of the law.

A few of them acknowledged Clint in some way, but most of them seemed to have more important matters on their minds. Clint belonged to that group, himself. As he walked into the courthouse, he turned to look at a sign displayed prominently over one of the biggest nearby doors which read:

ORIGIN COURTROOM NUMBER ONE
JUDGE HENRY KRUEGER PRESIDING

Yep, Clint thought as he headed toward that door. *Just the man I wanted to see.*

NINETEEN

Clint was approaching the door marked by Judge Krueger's sign when he was stopped by a mountain wearing a form-fitting black suit. The mountain scowled down at him and placed his hand on Clint's shoulder, which was all he needed to stop Clint in his tracks.

Although there was no way for Clint to miss a man who took up that much space, the guard had simply been standing so still that he blended in with all the other imposing statues nearby.

"Court's in session," the mountain said through a mouthful of crooked teeth.

Clint was taken aback for a moment by just how quickly the guard had moved. He reared up and did his best to stare the mountain straight in the eyes. "I need to see Judge Krueger."

"What about?"

"It's a matter I need to talk about with him. Not you. Not anyone else."

The mountain regarded Clint through eyes that displayed more than a fair share of intelligence. While most bulky guards tended to be just as dumb as the doors they stood in front of, this one seemed to have a little more going on upstairs.

"Well, the only ones Judge Krueger is talking to at the moment are in that courtroom. That's not you. Not anytime soon."

"When can I see him?"

"Never, if you plan on keeping that gun on. I could have you tossed out of here for going this far being heeled and all."

"All right then," Clint said, taking a more respectable tone. "When should I come back?"

Although the mountainous guard maintained his politeness, his voice was like the rumble of an earthquake rolling just beneath the ground. "Make an appointment."

Clint stepped back and looked around the courthouse's entryway. In his haste to get to the courtroom, he'd passed by a row of desks as well as several other smaller doors marked with names that hadn't struck Clint as the least bit familiar.

There was also a bit of commotion at the front door, since the mountain wasn't the only guard in the place. A few other men armed with pistols were approaching Clint after having been passed by like they didn't even exist. There were three in all, and they were whispering something among themselves while spreading out to walk shoulder to shoulder. They stopped about five paces from Clint and waited for the mountain to take the lead.

"First desk closest to the door," the mountain said, as if following Clint's exact train of thought. His voice was level and perfectly calm, which was a definite contrast to the concerned expressions worn by the other guards. "And if you try to storm in here wearing that gun," he added just as calmly, "I'll make you eat it."

Coming from anyone else, that statement might have sounded like bluster. But coming from the mouth of that mountain, it was unmistakably plain fact.

Rather than go against the current, Clint decided to play along. "Fine," he said with a tip of his hat. And that was all it took to get the mountain to back off a step and resume his stance in front of the door to Courtroom Number One.

The guards weren't Clint's enemies. So far, Clint wasn't even too sure about where Judge Krueger stood in the scheme of things. What he knew was that he needed to talk to Krueger about the note that had been tacked onto One-Thumb, and he needed to do so without getting tossed into a jail cell himself.

Pissing off a judge was never a good way to conduct business. If Krueger needed to be dealt with, it would be done without storming through a guard doing his job in the middle of a trial. Clint would make his appointment and act like a civilized man.

You could always catch more flies with honey than with vinegar.

Just because that saying was as old as the hills, and just as tired, didn't make it any less true. But it also didn't change the job that Clint had to do while in Origin. If he could finish it in a civilized way, he would do just that.

And when the time came for him to stop being civilized, an entire mountain range wouldn't stand in his way.

TWENTY

Clint's appointment was for later in the day. In the meantime, he took a little while to find a place for Eclipse and himself to spend the night. There were plenty of fine liveries in Origin, so Clint simply picked one that was closest to the hotel he'd chosen. As for the hotel, a bit more effort went into picking that.

Shifting his thinking to that of a scout, he regarded the town of Origin more as enemy territory. That way, he picked out possible trouble spots and a few places that he wanted to stay away from just in case trouble came looking for him. For most men, this might have been a little extreme. For Clint Adams, however, it was all too necessary.

The survey didn't take too long, because it wasn't even close to the first time he'd done it. Eventually, he settled on a quaint little place on the corner of Fifth and Main Streets called the Broken Banister. When he first stepped inside, Clint thought the place was closed or possibly not even a hotel at all. In fact, it looked more like someone's home.

The front room was mostly filled with bookshelves and a rack holding the most recent editions of the local newspaper. There were doors leading to other rooms on either side as well as a small square hole in the wall directly in front of Clint. That hole was covered with a wood panel, and when that panel slid suddenly up to reveal a wide, beaming face, Clint almost reached for his gun.

"Hello there," the face said.

The person looking through the panel was a smiling woman wearing small, round spectacles. Now that Clint had a chance to get a look at her, he could see that she was probably in her late thirties, but would always be mistaken for someone much older so long as she kept her hair pinned up at the back of her head.

"Oh, sorry about that," she said. "I didn't mean to startle you. I just heard someone come in and didn't want you to think this place was empty."

"No problem. It's just been a long day."

"Then you'll want one of our rooms. The beds are clean and soft and there's three meals served every day. Best deal in town."

"What about the room overlooking the corner right outside?" Clint asked. "Is that one available?"

She nodded without hesitation. "Sure enough. There's only one guest and he wanted quiet, so he's on the other end of the hall from there. I think he's a writer."

"Then I'll take the room with the view."

"It can get noisy," the clerk warned.

Clint smirked and replied, "I could probably sleep through cannon fire."

Smiling a bit too much at the little joke, the clerk disappeared from the open panel. The sounds of shuffling behind the wall reached Clint's ears, and before he could get up to the panel itself, the space was filled once again by the woman's smiling face.

"Just sign this," she said, handing a register through to Clint, "and I'll get your key. Breakfast is at seven. Dinner's at six, and if you'd like some lunch, someone here'll be happy to put something together for you."

"Sounds great."

Pulling back the register after Clint had signed it, the clerk glanced down at the open book and then pulled it back through to her side of the wall. "Here you go, Mr. Adams," she said, holding a key through to him. "Have a nice stay."

Clint's room was Number Four, which also just happened to be the last room at the end of the hall on the second floor. The room was a decent size and even had a bathtub in one corner. Of course, if Clint had gotten into that tub, his knees would have been up under his chin, but that was beside the point. The bed was covered in fresh linens and a hell of a lot better than sleeping on a horse blanket in the middle of a prairie.

After setting his bags down, Clint went straight to the window and pulled open the curtains that were drawn over the rectangular pane. Despite the pleasant weather and friendly people, something had been bugging Clint for the last several minutes. Even before he'd gotten into the hotel, that nagging little something was chewing at the corner of his brain like a tick.

He knew what it was. Clint had been followed more than enough to recognize the feeling of being watched. It was a vague chill that ran down a man's neck and made his trigger finger itch if it wasn't touching iron. Gazing down at the busy intersection, Clint couldn't see anything to catch his interest right away, but he kept his eyes roaming over the tops of buildings, people and wagons as daily life in Origin rolled on below him.

The clerk sure hadn't been lying when she said the room was noisy. Even with the window open just enough to let some air in, Clint was surrounded by noises of all sorts. There were voices, the clatter of wooden wheels and even the sound of animals circling his head. All of those noises ceased, however, when he spotted the man in black come to a stop and look straight at the hotel Clint had chosen.

The man looked to be just over six feet tall and was

dressed in a suit that was even fancier than those worn by most professional gamblers. In the daylight, the man's shirt was the color of bones that had been bleached in the desert sun. His coat and pants were the color of crude oil. Although most of his face was shielded by a wide-brimmed hat, his eyes were clear as crystal when he shifted them up to look into Clint's window.

Clint didn't pull the curtains open any farther, but he didn't close them either. Instead, he simply returned the man's stare and sized up the figure on the street just as well as he knew he, himself, was being inspected.

He didn't need to see a holster to know the man across the street was heeled. There was something about the way the man carried himself that was like a wildcat with its claws sheathed.

It didn't take long for Clint to place what seemed so familiar about the man. He'd seen one or two men dressed in a similar way back in the courthouse. What didn't set well with Clint at all was the fact that, even though he'd been on the lookout for someone following him, he hadn't spotted the man in black until now.

That meant the man was good.

It also meant Clint was just going to have to be better.

TWENTY-ONE

Clint felt naked as he walked back into the courthouse without his modified Colt strapped around his waist. The weight of the gun was not just familiar, but as much a part of him as the weight of his arms hanging from his shoulders. After the way he'd nearly barged into the courtroom earlier, however, Clint doubted he'd be let inside any other way.

The guards were still there, except for the mountain who'd been standing in front of Courtroom Number One. Two of the others surrounded him the moment he stepped inside, and patted him down to make sure he wasn't carrying any concealed weapons. Although the search wasn't the most pleasant thing in the world, Clint guessed it was his fault for charging in so hastily before.

"You done?" Clint asked the guard who was patting down his sides and arms. "Because you're going to have to at least buy me dinner if you want to get any closer."

The joke had no effect on the guard, but it did get him to back up a step. "Top of the stairs," the guard said once he was satisfied Clint wasn't heeled. "Turn right and head for the door at the end of the hall. You won't be able to miss it."

After conducting their search, the guards were more comfortable trying to fix mean eyes upon Clint as he walked by. Not in the mood for those kind of games, Clint let the others think what they wanted and started heading for a large stone staircase in the middle of the courthouse entrance.

Since it was approaching early evening, the courthouse wasn't nearly as filled with people as it had been when Clint had first arrived. The few people that Clint did see were on their way out or being escorted to a smaller set of doors by armed lawmen.

Clint's steps echoed throughout the building as he climbed the stairs. Despite the circumstances that had brought him there, Clint couldn't help but be impressed by the courthouse itself. The fine architecture extended to the second floor as well, which began with a balcony overlooking the entrance and led to a hallway and row of doors.

After turning right, Clint kept walking and soaking up every sight and sound that he could. Some of the open doors led to offices of other judges or possibly lawyers. Clint didn't know enough about that sort of thing to know what the pecking order might be, but it was plain to see that whoever had an office there had worked awfully hard to get there.

Every office Clint could see was almost as fancy as the rest of the building. There were polished wooden desks, leather-bound books and even statues in some cases. Every so often, someone would see him walking by and close a door before he could get a chance to hear what people inside were discussing.

Clint came to the end of the balcony and immediately stepped into another hall. Almost instantly, he could see the mountainous guard standing outside the door at the end. What caught his eye even more was the fact that the guard didn't look so huge compared to the door he was guarding.

Even if a man only had one of his senses working, he would have been able to tell that this door belonged to the most important man in the courthouse. The edges were engraved with intricate designs, and fine paintings hung on either side. The sound of Clint's steps, as well as every other sound, became muffled thanks to the more closed quarters, which reminded him of a library or rich man's study.

The scent of leather and polish hung so heavily in the air that it clung to the back of Clint's throat. When he finally came to a stop at the door, Clint could see that the carvings on the frame were actually raised sculptures that blended perfectly into the wall.

Standing solidly in place, the mountainous guard watched Clint every step of the way. His hands were folded in front of him and his feet appeared to be planted in the floor in front of the door, which was just as tall as him.

The guard nodded approvingly as he saw Clint walk closer. "The boys downstairs give you a hard time?"

"Not at all," Clint replied. "That is, unless we were courting. Other than that, yeah. I'd say they went above and beyond the call of duty."

The big man didn't go through extra lengths to try and look tough. He did just fine without trying too hard. He was relaxed enough to act civilly without being aggressive. "Well, don't get any ideas, because I'm going to have to check you over one more time before you see Judge Krueger."

Raising his arms, Clint said, "Go on and get it over with."

The mountain's hands moved quickly where they needed to go. At one point, Clint thought he was going to be lifted off his feet like a child by his father. But soon the guard stepped back and pushed open the huge door.

"Go on inside."

Clint nodded as he walked past the mountain, unsure if he was just being led straight into a trap. Just because the Colt wasn't handy didn't mean that he wasn't ready and able to handle anything that might come his way. But the door opened on oiled hinges and closed silently behind him without anything out of the ordinary taking place. Then again, the judge's chambers were anything but ordinary.

If the rest of the offices and rooms Clint had seen were fancy, Judge Krueger's chambers were something out of a palace. Just as much care had been taken when carving the walls of that room as had been taken when chiseling the intricate designs on the ornate entryway. Statues were carved straight into the walls, and even the mahogany desk was carved with matching works of art.

Looking around, Clint felt overwhelmed by all there was to see. Rather than study the wood and stone, he focused on the flesh and blood that sat in a throne-like chair behind the huge desk. Clint reached into his pocket, found the familiar contents and felt the same anger start churning inside of him.

"What can I do for you, Mr. Adams?" the man behind the desk asked.

"Simple," Clint said, pulling out the folded note that had been tacked onto One-Thumb Ambrose and tossing it onto the desk. "Explain this."

TWENTY-TWO

Judge Henry Krueger was a thick, solidly built man who looked like he belonged in a general's uniform at the head of an army instead of in a judge's robes. His neck was like a tree trunk made out of muscle and his arms were short but equally strong. A brushy white mustache covered his upper lip as well as most of his mouth, each whisker looking like a silver wire.

His skin was leathery and rough, which was a good match to his piercing, hardened eyes. Those eyes moved over Clint and sized him up in a second before darting down to the piece of parchment that had been thrown onto his desk.

"You're Clint Adams?" the judge asked, speaking as though he not only knew the answer already but was disappointed in it as well.

Clint stood in front of the judge's desk, sensing that the man on the other side of it expected him to sit down and hold his tone. "I am," Clint replied. "And that would make you Judge Krueger."

Even though it was plain to see that the judge was used to getting more respect from the people he let into his inner sanctum, he wasn't about to call Clint out about it. At least, not yet anyway.

"You created quite a stir earlier today," Krueger stated. "You know, it's not too hard to get a sit-down with some-one if you're having legal problems."

At that moment, Clint couldn't put his finger on what was angering him more: the bloody parchment that had brought him to Origin or the way Judge Krueger completely ignored it. "I'm not having legal problems," Clint said, wondering just how long the judge was prepared to act like nothing was wrong. "I wanted to have a word with you about something I found outside of Trickle Creek. You know the place?"

"Yes," Krueger said while furrowing his eyebrows in subtle concentration. "I believe I've been there once or twice on some matter or other."

A heavy silence filled the room when Clint refused to make any more small talk. For a moment, it seemed that Krueger was more than willing to sit and enjoy the quiet. Finally, he turned his gaze back down to the parchment. "What's this?"

"You should know what that is, Judge. It's got your name on it."

Without picking up the parchment, Krueger used the tip of his finger to turn it around so he could read the lettering. He nodded and then looked up again once he was through. "What was your question?"

"Is that sign correct?"

"Yes." Tapping a scribble at the bottom of the parchment, he said, "It has the signature of one of my constables."

"Your constables? Would these be the sort of constables that wear hoods over their faces, perhaps? Or maybe pillowcases?"

"What is that supposed to mean?"

"This man was swinging from a tree in the middle of nowhere. This note," Clint said, stabbing one finger onto the parchment, "was stuck onto that man's chest using tacks. That's his blood right there."

"Do you carry some sort of rank that I should know about, Mr. Adams? Because I fail to see why I should listen to you questioning my method of upholding the law."

"This is a pretty big town," Clint said. "For that matter, Trickle Creek isn't too bad. Either place should have a gallows, along with witnesses and all the other things that come along with a legal hanging. Seeing a man swinging from a tree with a note tacked through his skin makes me wonder just how legal this hanging was. And just so you know, an illegal hanging is called murder."

"I know what an illegal hanging is, Mr. Adams." Where Krueger's voice had been cool and level, it was now fiery and bearing a sharp edge. The temper that had shone through for those last few words was quickly subdued, however, and Judge Krueger forced himself back to a more reserved level.

"Those proclamations are left there for a reason, Mr. Adams. If there's a problem with one of my constables, I'll thank you for bringing it to my attention and then take care of it myself. Now, if that's all you had for me, I'll bid you good evening."

"That's not all I had for you," Clint said. "I'd like to know what that man did to warrant getting strung up and tortured like that."

"Tortured? I assure you nothing of the sort happened."

"All right then. I'll string you up from one of these rafters and knock some tacks through your chest. I bet that would be considered one hell of a way to torture someone."

Krueger shrugged and spread his open hands in front of him. "Disrespect for the dead, perhaps."

"The man I found wasn't dead," Clint said, watching Krueger carefully to see what kind of reaction he was going to get.

The judge twitched so slightly that most men would have missed it. But Clint was a poker player, and if he saw that twitch in a game, he would know without a doubt that Krueger was looking at some real ugly cards.

"What?" Krueger asked.

"He's not dead," Clint repeated. "That is, unless one of your constables got to him by now."

Krueger scowled as though he'd caught a whiff of fresh shit. Pushing back from his desk, he walked over to a set of books that were all the size of the hotel register Clint had signed not too long ago. "What's this man's name?" Krueger asked impatiently.

"Jeremiah Ambrose. He also goes by One-Thumb."

Krueger stopped with his fingers resting on one of the ledger-sized books and turned to look at Clint with a spark in his eye. "Oh, I remember that one. Were you here for his trial?"

"No."

"Do you even know what he did to wind up in my court?"

"Enlighten me."

"Mr. Ambrose is a horse thief. I'm sure someone like you can appreciate how serious that crime is. In fact, I'm surprised that anyone has to ask why a horse thief would wind up with his head in a noose. We simply can't tolerate that sort of thing."

Clint nodded. "True. But wouldn't someone from a court as grand as this one carry out their sentences more officially?"

"Mr. Adams, not every place has a gallows. There are plenty of jurisdictions where the same thing would have happened in precisely the same fashion."

"Not precisely. In fact, I've never seen something like that note before. Men hung by the order of a judge are done so in the middle of town. This one was carried out like a murder. It was out of the way and kept out of sight. Not even his wife knew what happened, and that leads me to believe that there wasn't much of a trial. At least, not a public one."

"Oh, is that a fact? Well, up to this point I've paid you the courtesy of hearing you out, but there's no reason for me to explain myself to you or anyone else."

Nodding toward the ledgers, Clint asked, "Could I see the records of the trial?"

"If you want to see them, fill out a petition. My patience with you has come to an end." With that, Krueger walked back behind his desk and stood with his fingertips pressed against the polished wood. "I trust you can find your own way out of my chambers."

"Aren't those files a matter of public record?"

"Yes, but to see them you must notify the proper people. See the clerks downstairs and I'm sure they'll be able to point you in the right direction. And before you say one more word," Krueger added, "remember just who it is you're talking to. I'm not some drunk in a bar who's afraid of your reputation as a gunfighter. I'm the highest judge in these parts and I don't have to take orders from the likes of you."

"I wasn't trying to give orders," Clint said plainly. "Just trying to get some answers to something that struck me as pretty damn rotten."

"Well, if you don't like the way I dispense my judgments, then perhaps you should move along to some other part of the country." With that, Krueger stomped his foot on the floor and dropped down into his padded chair.

Clint nodded, tipped his hat and turned to leave the room through the huge, ornate door. Even without getting a look at any records, he had learned a hell of a lot from his talk with Judge Krueger. Up until now, he'd had a bad feeling about what had happened to One-Thumb and suspected there was something else lurking below the surface. Now, however, he knew there was more. A lot more.

Unfortunately, he didn't know that Krueger's foot had found a knob built into the floor behind his desk and was tapping out a signal to the men waiting in the room below.

TWENTY-THREE

The room wasn't nearly as grand as most of the others in the courthouse. Although it was comfortable and quiet, it wasn't much more than four walls surrounding a few chairs and several racks of guns. At first glance, it would be easy to overlook the room's main entrance, which was a door recessed into the wall so well that even the cracks were barely visible.

The main thing that stood out in the room, apart from the weapons, was the bell hanging from the ceiling. That silver bell hung from a small rack and was only rung by a rope which hung down through a hole that had been drilled through the floor of the room above. Both of the men sitting in the room jumped from their seats as though their tails had been set on fire the instant that bell was rung.

Neither of them had to be told what to do when they heard that. If they knew how to get into that room at all, they would know what the sound of that bell meant.

"Jesus, it's about time," Lou Garner said as he placed his hand on a panel in the wall and pushed it inward. "I thought I was gonna be spending the night in here."

After a muted click within the wall, the door popped out a bit and then swung open on well-oiled hinges. The man next to Lou was Spencer Wilde, and the whiskers on his face were still nothing even close to being considered a beard.

"Don't speak too soon, Lou," Wilde said. "You may be spending the night in here after all. You know the judge. I wouldn't have been surprised if he walled you up in here for a week after how you pissed him off."

Lou turned on his heels and stuck a finger in Wilde's face. "I may take shit off of the judge, but I don't take none from nobody else. That sure as hell includes you, boy."

"All right, all right. But if we don't get moving, we'll both be locked up in here for good. That, or worse."

As angered as Lou may have been, he knew that the younger man was speaking the truth. Choking back whatever else he wanted to say, he stepped through the door and headed down the short hall that joined up with the public section of the courthouse. Wilde followed right behind him, making sure the door to the secret room was properly shut and locked.

The moment Lou stepped out of the hall, he was spotted by someone else dressed in the same tailored black suit worn by himself and Wilde.

Deke Gray stood with his back to the wall, facing out to all the courthouse entrances. His piercing eyes narrowed slightly when he saw Lou and Wilde emerge from the little hallway, and he immediately moved to intercept them.

"What's going on?" Deke asked in a scratchy whisper meant for only his two partners' ears.

Without sparing a glance toward Deke, Lou looked up toward the second-floor balcony. "Judge's alarm went off. Where's Marcus?"

"Still scouting."

Lou took a deep breath and put his hand on his side to make sure his gun was still hanging beneath his coat. "You think this is about Adams?"

Deke nodded once. "He was the last one to head up there."

"Then shouldn't we wait for Marcus?" Wilde asked. "I mean, that is Clint Adams up there, not just some—"

"If you want to wait, you sit back there and wait, boy," Lou snarled. Before he could continue his threat, he spotted a figure striding onto the balcony from the second-floor chambers. The moment he caught sight of Clint's face, Lou's first instinct was to turn toward the stone stairs. "Is that him?"

"Yeah," Deke replied. "That's him."

TWENTY-FOUR

When Clint left the judge's chambers, he fully expected to get some trouble from the hulking guard outside the door. Much to his surprise, however, he got nothing more than a nod and a stern glance from the mountain as he passed by. The man didn't even follow him as Clint headed down the hall.

Just because the trouble didn't come right away, however, didn't mean that it wasn't coming at all. Clint still kept his eyes and ears open, while keeping his hand close to the holster at his side. His stomach tightened into a knot for a moment when he realized once again that he was without the Colt altogether. Despite the fact that he knew exactly where the weapon was, it might as well have been at the bottom of an unmarked grave for all the good it would do him.

Clint walked out onto the balcony overlooking the courthouse's main entrance and moved straight for the stairs. There were even fewer people around, which made the men in black stand out even more than they already did.

Although he couldn't quite see their faces, Clint recognized the way they were dressed, as well as the manner in which they carried themselves. They might not have in-

cluded the same man he'd spotted outside his hotel, but
they were in the same group. Anything else would have
been too much of a coincidence for him to swallow.

Keeping his eyes facing forward and his steps quick,
Clint went down the stairs and headed for the front door.
All of his attention was focused on those men standing at
the entrance. One of them, a younger man with a face full
of uneven whiskers, was looking right at him. The others
were apparently watching the street outside.

Suddenly, the door to Clint's left smashed open and
people of all ages came streaming out. It must have been
the last case being heard for the day, because the courthouse seemed otherwise empty. But that same case must
have been pretty important, because there were a hell of a
lot of people leaving the room.

"This is bullshit!" a man screamed as he was dragged
from the room by a pair of lawmen. "I didn't do anything!
Nobody proved a damn thing!"

Everyone coming out of the courtroom seemed to be
reading from that same page. Everyone, that is, except for
the men dragging the accused kicking and screaming
toward the door. But rather than take him into the room
where Clint had seen other prisoners taken, this one was
dragged straight to the men in black.

All three of the darkly dressed figures turned to get a
look at what was being brought to them. Just then, they
stepped aside and let another man in black step past them
to take the prisoner by the shackles binding his wrists.

Clint recognized that face immediately as the man
who'd been watching him from outside his hotel. Apparently, the man recognized Clint as well, because he fixed
his eyes on him and gave a quick nod.

Once again, Clint got the feeling that something very,
very wrong was happening right in front of him, and
though he wasn't about to interfere with a legal proceed-

ing, Clint wasn't about to let someone else get lynched either.

Any other time and Clint might have just figured the screaming man was another poor asshole who was paying for his deeds. But after all he'd seen so far, Clint didn't have one bit of faith in Origin's brand of justice.

Clint stepped up to the lawmen taking the screaming man away and said, "Hold on a minute. Where are you taking this man?"

The lawman looked Clint up and down and kept walking past him. "Don't worry about it."

"Aren't the holding cells over that way?" Clint asked, nodding toward the smaller doors not too far from the stone staircase.

Both guards looked over that way and then back at Clint. The expression on their faces was identical and they reeked of guilt.

"Just step back and let us by," the first guard said.

But Clint's words had not only done their job, but had spread throughout the rest of the crowd. At first, the angry people coming out of the courtroom had looked at Clint as though they didn't know what to make of him. Now they pumped their fists in the air and started lending their own voices to his cause.

"He's right. I been here before," one of the crowd members said. "The jail cells are back the other way! Where are you takin' him?"

"Yeah! Where are you takin' him?" someone else shouted.

The man in custody struggled even harder against the lawmen. "They're gonna kill me! All because Judge Krueger wants me out of his way! Just like they did to all the others! Just like they did to—"

The man's words were cut brutally short by the impact of a pistol butt against his jaw. The pistol was in the hand of the man in black that had followed Clint to his hotel.

And when that blow landed, it silenced the entire crowd just as effectively as it had silenced the man in custody.

Deke stepped forward and took hold of the man's arm as he wavered on his feet. "All of you settle down!" he ordered. "This man is going to be taken care of by the letter of the law."

"Yeah," someone shouted from the back of the crowd. "Krueger's law."

"*The* law," Deke snarled. "There ain't but one kind in this country." Although he didn't say anything else after that, his eyes did a whole lot of talking. As they panned around to each face in the crowd, those eyes gave a command to shut up and step back before they got hurt. Everyone who saw them not only understood the message in those eyes, but obeyed it instantly.

"Marcus," Deke said to the man in black who now had hold of the prisoner. "Take this man to the holding cells."

That order was carried out as well, and the man in black who'd followed Clint earlier dragged the prisoner farther into the courthouse, toward the smaller doors in the back. Clint started to follow, but was stopped by an iron grip around his left arm.

"Not you," Lou growled while pulling Clint toward the front door. "You come along with us."

Clint left with the other black-clad men through the front door. At that moment, he didn't really have much choice.

TWENTY-FIVE

As Clint was led out the front door, not one member of the crowd said or did a thing. It was as if invisible hands were pushing the crowd back. The fear in their eyes was so strong that it could be felt like a wet fog in the air. Plenty of them looked like they wanted to step in, and the rest merely looked like they pitied Clint. None of them, however, were about to risk trading places with him.

"For a town as cosmopolitan as this," Clint said as he was dragged outside and down the steps leading to the street, "the way you treat newcomers sure leaves a lot to be desired."

"Shut yer mouth," Lou snarled.

Clint turned to look at the stout man directly. "What's the matter, Lou? Still having woman troubles?"

"You son of a bitch."

When he said those words, Lou made the very mistake that Clint had been hoping for. He went to spin Clint around to face him head-on. It was a simple action, but accomplished two very important things in Clint's view. First of all, it caused Lou to readjust his grip on Clint's arm, which required him to shift his fingers for half of a moment. And second, it gave Clint a bit of momentum to add to his own as he spun around twice as quickly as Lou was pushing him.

With both of those things working in his favor, Clint was able to take back some of the control the men in black were obviously used to having. When he felt that momentary bit of weakness as Lou shifted his fingers, Clint snapped his arm out of the man's grip. Using the momentum from Lou's shove, Clint only had to snap his arm out to crack his knuckles into Lou's face like a whip.

"Oh, sorry about that," Clint said for the benefit of anyone else watching the exchange.

With Lou still reeling back from the startling jab, Clint turned his back on the men and started walking down the stairs on his own. Before he could make it down one more step, he felt another hand clamp around his arm like a sprung bear trap.

This hand wasn't as clumsy and brutish as Lou's. This one was crisp and precise, locking around Clint expertly in a way that didn't give him any openings to work against.

"You'll come along with us, Adams," Deke hissed into Clint's ear. "Otherwise we'll let you go and gun you down for trying to escape lawful custody."

All Clint had to do was take a quick survey of the men in black to see that they meant business. Each of them had his hand near his gun. The only difference among them was that one seemed ready to draw right then instead of at Deke's first command. But no matter how much he wanted to clear leather, Lou held fast and kept his trembling hand at bay.

"You want to test us some more or do you want to come along and hear what we got to say?" Deke asked.

Clint walked where he was being led. "Maybe it's something in the water, but people tend to have real short tempers around here," Clint said.

"Maybe we just don't take to smart-asses like yourself questioning the way we do things."

With Deke setting the pace, the entire group was moving quickly. In fact, they were already at the bottom of the steps and turning away from the boardwalk.

"I'm surprised more people don't question you," Clint said. "The way you do things doesn't seem to be too popular."

"It works."

"Yeah, but for just you and the judge, or everyone?"

Clint didn't get an answer to that one.

"All I wanted to do was check on that note you left," Clint said.

Wilde was bringing up the rear of the group, but he was close enough to hear every word. "What note?" he asked.

Without taking his eyes from Clint, Deke replied, "The note left on that son of a bitch we hung outside of Trickle Creek."

"One-Thumb? I thought he was missing."

"Shut the fuck up, Wilde," Deke snarled. "I knew those notes were a damn fool idea."

Clint could detect every emotion that was tacked onto the other men's words just as surely as he'd seen that note tacked onto One-Thumb's chest. "You don't like the way Judge Krueger does things, do you?"

Clint could feel the grip around his arm tightening, which was just as good as any spoken reply.

"You prefer to shoot a man in the skull, drop him in a hole and be done with it?" Clint asked.

"Tell you what," Deke said. "Why don't I just let you find out firsthand?"

TWENTY-SIX

Clint knew he was in for trouble the moment Deke started shoving him toward a small, empty building a few doors down from the courthouse. The building wasn't much more than a shack and appeared to have been a store of some kind when it was in its prime. There was a counter and several long tables that were covered with layers of dust.

He also knew better than to expect anyone in the area to do anything as simple as cast a suspicious eye their direction. Clint saw too much fear in the faces of the locals to expect anything from them. But that wasn't necessarily a bad thing in Clint's mind. It just meant he wouldn't have anyone tripping him up when it was time for him to move.

Deke shoved him into the abandoned store with enough force to break the door if it hadn't already been hanging off its hinges. He didn't say a word. Instead, he just stepped in behind Clint and gave one more shove to put Clint a few paces in front of him.

Lou was next to enter the store, and his eyes were those of a hungry animal closing in on a piping hot steak. "You think you're pretty tough, don't you, Adams? Well, you ain't shit to me. You got that?"

Lou's bluster fell upon deaf ears. Clint was too busy sizing up his situation. For the most part, it wasn't good. He was quickly being surrounded by three armed men, at least two of whom were all but unknowns to him. He was also in enemy territory, and judging by the bloodstains on the floor, it was territory that was used for bad purposes fairly often.

Wilde was the last one in. He shut the door behind him and placed his hand upon the grip of his pistol. Although he looked nervous, there was an anxiousness in his face that meant he was the type to draw and fire rather than turn tail and run when he was spooked.

"Shut up, Lou," Deke snarled. Turning his attention back to Clint, he said, "Judge Krueger don't need to explain himself to you or anyone else. Ever. You got that?"

Clint didn't answer. Instead, he shuffled back until his heels bumped up against the bottom of the counter. At least now he had something solid to his back.

Deke stopped just outside of kicking or punching range. His feet squared off and planted themselves into a solid firing stance. "You got one way out of this, Adams. Tell us where Ambrose got to and we'll let you walk out of here. I won't bother lying to you, so I'll tell you that you'll be hurting when you do leave, but you'll leave."

"What's my other choice?" Clint asked, just to buy himself some time to get a better feel for his surroundings.

"Your other choice is to die here and tack on another day or two to the work we got ahead of us. That's it."

Clint let the silence in the store build up. Outside, there were sounds of normal daily life, but it might as well have been a hundred miles away. Whether or not anyone knew what was going on inside the store, there wasn't anyone willing to come within ten yards of the place.

Silence, however, wasn't the only thing building up. Tension flowed off of Lou like waves of heat off the desert floor. Clint could feel it getting stronger and could see the man's fists clenching, as well as the muscles in his jaw squirming beneath his skin.

Clint waited for another couple seconds, which was all he dared for the moment. Wilde's hand was closing tighter around his gun and Lou seemed ready to crack at any second. Only Deke kept his resolve, but he was a hard man to read anyhow.

"So the judge pays you to be his gunmen," Clint said. "Is that it? What's he getting out of it?"

Deke's eyes narrowed. "Just tell me where Ambrose went."

Shifting his gaze toward Lou, Clint could tell that he'd let just the right amount of time crawl by. The man was practically jumping out of his skin. "Hey, Lou," Clint said. "You might want to know that no matter how badly I look after this, Misty's still going to think you're uglier than a skunk's ass."

A single twitch worked its way through Lou's entire face. It started at his fists, worked its way up through his chest and neck and then started tugging at every muscle from his jawline up past his forehead. By the time the twitch had run its course, Lou's eyes were filled with the kind of rage saved only for rabid dogs.

"You son of a goddamn whore" were the last coherent words to come out of Lou's mouth before he charged toward Clint.

Wilde was so shocked by the sudden outburst of hatred that all he could do was try and stay out of the way. Although Deke was still in control of himself, there was no way he could pull the reins on Lou before it was too late.

Now that he'd called down the thunder, Clint braced himself for it. He backed up against the counter and reached down to take hold of it with both hands. Crouching slightly at the knees and waist, he held his ground as Lou came stampeding straight for him.

The man may have been shorter than Clint, but Lou's

bulk was enough to give him a powerful head of steam as he threw all of his emotions into his charge. His hands reached out for Clint, shoving Deke aside as he tried to get in his way. All he could see was Clint's face through the red haze that clouded his mind. All Lou could think about was closing his fingers around Clint's neck.

Every bit of common sense within Clint's skull told him to get the hell out of Lou's way by any means possible. The look in the other man's eyes alone was enough to get Clint thinking about the fastest way out of that building. But he knew his chances of getting out of that store were next to nothing, especially since the men in black surely already knew every nook and cranny of the place.

Clint pushed those thoughts and instincts aside. Instead, he stood right in front of that stampede until he spotted his single best chance to get away. That chance came when Lou was almost within arm's reach and started to extend his hand toward Clint's neck.

At the last possible moment, Clint ducked straight down while bringing his right hand up. He hoped to grab hold of Lou's wrist and keep hold of it for just a second or two. Although the man was moving wildly, Clint managed to snag his wrist and lock his fingers tightly in place around it.

A shot was fired from the front of the store, and Clint didn't have to look to know it had been the youngest of the men who'd finally lost his composure. The bullet whipped through the air over both Clint's and Lou's heads and dug a tunnel into a nearby wall.

Still keeping hold of Lou's wrist, but already losing his grip, Clint twisted his body around and out of Lou's path just as he felt rough fingers graze along his throat. Lou's nails took a chunk of meat from Clint's neck, but didn't do much damage.

Already, Lou was twisting around to get another chance at him. Lou's teeth were bared and spit flew from his mouth as he let out a savage, brutish growl. Somehow, he'd gotten a knife into his left hand and was pulling that arm back before stabbing forward.

Clint hadn't seen Lou draw the knife, but he saw the glint of steel just in time to do something about it. His entire body strained as he moved to get out of the way of Lou's blade. The knife hissed through the air, sent a pinching pain through Clint's right side and then slammed into the top of the counter.

As blood trickled down Clint's neck, he heard the sound of guns clearing leather and saw both Wilde and Deke taking aim at him.

Now it was going to get really interesting.

TWENTY-SEVEN

Although Clint's first impulse was to reach for his Colt, he knew damn well that it wasn't there. The thought to draw his weapon only lasted a fraction of a second, since the rest of him was in the process of dealing with the other guns in the room.

Having knocked Lou into the counter, Clint was able to buy himself a few precious moments. That time, however, was already up and Lou was taking another swing at him with his blade. Clint reflexively dodged first one swing and then another, which came in frenzied succession.

Clint wound up with his back against the counter as Wilde took another shot at him. The youngest man in black was still nervous, but he was pulling it together well enough for Clint to start worrying about him. Deke was still his main concern, though, and Clint was watching that one like a hawk even as he dealt with Lou.

"I'm gonna kill you," Lou snarled as he threw himself at Clint. He brought his knife stabbing down again as he came, letting out a breath that sounded like a gust coming from a bellows.

Clint snapped a jab into Lou's gut and kept his fist there to push all the air from his lungs. Although the move took

108

an extra second or two, it was worth it when he felt Lou crumple around his fist like a puppet with its strings cut.

The pounding of footsteps filled the abandoned store. Without looking, Clint knew the hurried ones belonged to Wilde while the steady tapping ones were Deke's. Wilde took a shot, but this time the bullet almost took a piece from Lou's hide since he was the one to wheel around and face Clint straight on.

Clint stayed as close as he could to Lou for as long as possible before the shorter man violently pushed him back. When he saw Lou flip the blade in his hand to get in better stabbing position, Clint lifted his right leg and slammed the tip of his boot into the bottom of Lou's wrist.

Lou's face contorted in pain and his fingers reflexively opened, allowing the blade to clatter to the floor. Without a moment's pause, he reached for his holster and went to draw the iron waiting there. Suddenly, the pained expression disappeared. It was replaced by one of pure shock.

"What the hell?" Lou grunted.

His holster was empty.

Clint brought up his arm to take aim with the gun that he'd stolen while in such close proximity to Lou. He only had to wait for the space of a heartbeat before Lou made his final mistake.

Still fueled by rage, Lou snapped his hand around to the small of his back where he kept his stash of sharpened steel. The throwing knife he had there wasn't as big as the blade laying on the floor, but he'd killed plenty of men with it and intended on killing at least one more.

Clint saw Lou make the reach and still waited. Not even a second had passed since he'd lifted his gun, but in the middle of a fight, every breath seemed to take an hour. Recognizing the glint of steel being bared, Clint stepped back with one foot, so his side was facing Lou. At the same time, he aimed and fired the gun in his hand, sending a bullet straight through Lou's forehead.

The impact of the shot snapped Lou's head back with sickening force. His arm still managed to flick the throwing knife toward Clint, and the sharpened steel turned through the air less than an inch from Clint's chest. If Clint hadn't reflexively shifted into his sideways stance, Lou might very well have had the last laugh.

As it was, the blade stuck into a windowpane and Lou dropped with his brains forming a red mist behind him.

With Lou on the floor, Clint could now see the rest of the store which had been previously blocked from view. Apparently, he hadn't been the only one to position himself strategically, since Clint got a nasty surprise after Lou fell backward.

Deke had been standing behind Lou and couldn't be seen by Clint until this very moment. Even so, Clint spotted Deke, on one knee in a low firing stance, in time to shift his aim in that direction. Two shots were fired so closely together that they almost sounded like a single blast. One shot came before the other, however, and unfortunately that shot was Deke's.

Clint felt a sharp pain in his gun hand that sent a wave of fire up his entire arm. He knew his own shot wasn't going to hit its mark even as he fired it. But he pulled his trigger all the same, which was enough to keep Deke from firing again.

The pain in Clint's hand was followed by a numbness and then the thump of his gun hitting the floor. Clint didn't have much say in the matter since the grazing shot had caused his hand to twitch open reflexively. Rather than stand and fret about dropping his gun, Clint dropped right after it. He squatted down and rolled back, snatching the pistol from the floor as he rolled over it. When he came to a stop, he was on one knee as well and aiming at Deke.

At least, he would have been aiming at Deke if the man had still been there. Clint blinked a few times to clear the rush of blood through his head, brought about by the excitement as well as the injuries he'd sustained. Although there was a heavy shroud of smoke hanging in the air, it was obvious that Clint was alone with Lou's body in that store.

Keeping himself low, he avoided the windows while making his way to the front door. When he got there, Clint saw only one figure walking down the street.

Deke either heard Clint coming or simply knew he would be along shortly, because he turned and fixed his piercing gaze on him directly. Coming to a stop in the street, which was all but empty, Deke kept his hand over the grip of his pistol, which had already been dropped into its holster.

As much as he wanted to finish what had begun, Clint knew there was more than one man in black out there. The youngest of the group may have been a bit shaky, but he might very well find some resolve after setting up an ambush with Deke as the bait. Plus, there was still the man who'd followed Clint to his hotel. If he could go that far without being spotted, he could very well be setting his sights on Clint at that very moment.

Sometimes, there was a good reason to purposely walk into a trap. This wasn't one of them. Clint stepped back into the store and shut the door behind him.

TWENTY-EIGHT

Clint's pride wasn't the only thing stinging him when he got back to his hotel. Leaving that fight unfinished would sting a bit longer than the rest of the wounds he'd gotten. He got his share of awkward glances as he swiped away the blood trickling from his neck while he walked down the street. By the time he stepped into the lobby of his hotel, Clint's hands and shirtsleeves were covered in blood.

"Is that you, Mr. Adams?" the woman behind the panel in the front room asked. "I heard that—"

"I'm fine," Clint interrupted as politely as he could. "Could I get some water sent up to my room?"

Still straining to get a better look at him as he walked up the stairs, the clerk almost stuck her head completely through her hole in the wall. "Sure. I'll get that right away. I'll bring it myself."

Clint heard most of that before getting to his room, unlocking the door and stepping inside. The first thing he reached for was the holster slung over his bedpost. The familiar leather slid through his hands and around his waist so smoothly that he barely even felt it. He definitely felt the weight of the gun at his side once the holster was fastened, and it was a most welcome feeling indeed.

Only once the Colt was securely in place did Clint look down at his hands. They were covered in dust, which was stuck to his skin by a thick layer of sticky blood. It was as if the sight of the blood brought the injuries back to him, and Clint felt the stinging sensations once again at his neck.

Rummaging through his saddlebags, Clint quickly found a small shaving mirror which he used to get a closer look at where he'd been hurt. There was no question that there was a good amount of blood. What he soon discovered, however, was that most of that blood had gotten there after being smeared over his skin by his own hands.

A few tentative touches told him where the real wounds were and that they weren't even bad enough to fret over.

A knocking came on his door, which sounded like a bunch of nervous squirrels banging their heads against the wood. The knocks were tentative at first, but soon took on a stronger, more tenacious tone.

"Mr. Adams," came the clerk's squeaky voice. "I've got that water for you."

Clint only had to lean forward to reach the door handle from where he was, and he opened it to let the woman inside. As soon as she got a look at him, the clerk's eyes widened and she pulled in a worried breath. For a moment, it looked as if she might even let the water basin she was holding slip from her hands.

"Oh, my goodness," she gasped. "Are you all right? I heard that something happened at the courthouse, but I didn't know it was this bad."

Clint reached out and took the water basin from her before it wound up shattered on the floor. "I'm doing just fine," he assured her. "It looks a lot worse than it is."

"Well, it looks pretty bad. Let me see."

Before Clint could say anything else, he was practically shoved back onto his bed so the clerk could walk by. She went straight to the little table where Clint had put the water basin and proceeded to pull open one of the drawers that Clint hadn't even known was there.

"I heard there was shooting down the street," she said, pulling a washcloth from the little drawer and dunking it into the water.

"Yeah, a bit."

Glancing over to him to take another look at his wounds, she asked, "Did you get shot?"

"No, nothing so bad as that."

"Thank the Lord. There's enough people getting hurt around here without adding a nice man like you to the mix."

"Are there a lot of shootings around here?" Clint asked, watching the clerk closely for her reaction.

She paused for a moment with her hands in the water, but quickly resumed twisting the cloth until it was properly soaked. "Not any more than any other town, I guess. Origin's getting big and you can't exactly choose the types of folks that come here."

"Not really."

Taking a breath, she wrapped the wet cloth around her hand and gently reached out to wipe away the blood from Clint's face. "Here you go," she said softly. "Let's clean you up to see what we can see. You may need to go to a doctor."

"That won't be necessary."

"And how do you know?" she asked, regaining some of her previous good humor. "Do you practice a lot of medicine?"

"No, but I spend a lot of time where it isn't safe to be."

Some of the shine left her smile, but that was just because it was replaced by something deeper. The clerk continued to clean and dab with the cloth, but now she was watching him extra closely, as if there was a lot going on inside her head.

"Well," she said, "I guess someone's got to spend time there. Otherwise the rest of us wouldn't be so safe."

Clint never expected to be rewarded for the things he did. Most of the time, he did them because they were the proper things to do and he was the proper man to do them. Certainly, rewards came along with his efforts every now and then, but there were other things that made doing them worthwhile.

The subtle, grateful smile on the clerk's face was most definitely one of those things.

"What's your name?" Clint asked.

The clerk looked surprised to hear that question, but then lowered her eyes and focused on what she was doing with the washcloth. "Joan."

Clint put his finger under Joan's chin and lifted her face so he could look directly into her eyes. "Thanks, Joan."

"It's hardly anything. Just some water and a few moments of my time."

"It's a lot more than that." And then Clint kissed her. It wasn't exactly planned, but he simply went with what felt right and wound up with his lips pressed against hers.

Joan's cheeks flushed as she pulled away, but her smile remained. In fact, her smile grew with every second that she spent in his room.

TWENTY-NINE

The men in black retrieved Lou's body and dragged it out of the abandoned store without getting more than half a sideways glance from anyone else. They took the body to the undertaker's without a word and then continued along their way.

Deke had been the leader of the small group since it was first brought together, and he'd seen plenty of other members come and go. For now, he was glad to have the group trimmed down to three. He figured he could go a lot farther without any more dead weight holding them back.

"So that's that," Wilde said. "Which of us gets to tell the judge?"

Having returned from the courthouse, Marcus stood silently next to Deke. His eyes were in constant motion, taking in everything around him, as well as the other two men in the group.

"We don't tell him anything," Deke said. "He'll find out soon enough. We still got a job to do."

"You ain't mad about what happened to Lou?" Wilde asked.

"Mad?" Deke scoffed. "Hell, I expected him to get himself killed before too long. I been expecting it ever since he started going so crazy over that singer. It ain't healthy to get so involved like that with any woman."

"Lou's not the only one with that problem," Marcus said, the words coming from him like fog seeping up from the ground. When he spoke, his lips barely moved enough to shift the thick goatee covering his mouth.

Deke turned slightly to look at the third man. Marcus stood just over six feet tall and had a lean, muscular build. He had mean eyes that caused most folks to look away from him almost immediately. His skin was pale and seemed downright chalky in contrast to the deep blackness of his clothes.

"What's that mean?" Deke asked.

"It means that Adams has a soft spot for women, too. Maybe not soft enough to make him as stupid as Lou, but it's there. I seen it when he came to town in the company of that blonde."

Nodding, Deke mulled that over for a second.

"There's a woman working at the hotel where he's staying," Marcus added.

Perking up a bit, Deke asked, "Was he making eyes at her, too?"

"Couldn't say for certain, but he seems like the sort to try and protect any woman so long as he thinks she's just some innocent bystander."

Wilde couldn't hold his tongue any longer. Leaning in as if he thought someone was watching them, he said, "She is innocent. I know the lady that works at the hotel Marcus tracked Adams to and she doesn't have anything to do with any of this."

Both Marcus and Deke shifted their gaze toward Wilde. They regarded him silently and intently enough to make Wilde back up a step. Their stares were similar to those of predators picking out which member of their pack was the next to drop.

"You going soft now?" Deke asked. "After all we done, you decide to go soft here and now?"

"Innocent don't matter, kid," Marcus said. "If you didn't learn that by now, you might never learn it."

Puffing out his chest, Wilde said, "I'm not going soft. All I'm saying is that the lady at that hotel isn't a part of this until Judge Krueger points her out to us. Until then, there's no need to do anything to her or anyone else for that matter. He's the one who—"

Deke's hands shot out so quickly that neither of the two others saw them coming. They snapped forward so his hands could clamp around the front of Wilde's coat and pull him in so fast that the youngest man in black was almost yanked from his boots.

"Krueger isn't here right now," Deke snarled. "I am. You're not the one who gets the orders direct from the judge's mouth. I am. And you're not the one to make orders. I am. Is that clear enough for you?"

"Y-yeah, Deke. I was just—"

"Save it," Deke interrupted. "Just nod your head if you understand what I'm saying to you."

Having taken a moment to catch his breath, Wilde was starting to feel anger set in after being called out in such a way in front of Marcus and anyone else who happened to be watching. Even if nobody was watching, Wilde would have been just as mad. But he sucked it up and nodded all the same.

"Good." Deke let the younger man go. "Judge Krueger keeps us on to enforce his rulings, whether they're in or out of that courthouse. He tells me what needs to be done and I pass those orders on to you. How we go about it is up to us. The judge doesn't have a problem with how we work, and if he's behind us, there ain't nobody else in town to question us.

"The job we got now is to take care of Adams. We all know what the bell in the judge's chambers is for. We hear it and we take care of whoever comes through that door. If we don't, we failed our duty, and if we fail, the judge finds four more men to take our jobs."

Focusing on Wilde, Deke said, "I didn't like seeing Lou die any more than you did. But Lou was stupid and wasn't thinking about what we aim to do. If someone like Adams comes poking around in the wrong places, all that we been working for will come out and it'll all be over. We need to get Adams before he finds out enough to cause some real damage and we need to do it in the quickest way possible."

Now Deke shifted his eyes toward the other man in black, who still had yet to move from his original spot. "Marcus, you've been the one following Adams. What do you think is the best way to get to him?"

"That singer from Trickle Creek is working at the Neapolitan. He's sweet on her. That woman at his hotel is sweet on him. Either one of them gets hurt and Adams will come running."

"You certain about that?"

Even after glancing toward Wilde to see the look in his eyes, Marcus nodded. "Yeah. It's either that or wait for him to find us, and I've heard enough to know we don't want the Gunsmith coming after us."

"All right then," Deke said with a nod. "Let's get this taken care of before Adams finds out what's really set to happen in this town."

THIRTY

It was getting late and the area around the Broken Banister hotel was all but deserted. Every so often, a straggler or two would wander by, but they would quickly find where they needed to be and disappear from view. Most of the activity in town was confined to the entertainment districts scattered here and there, leaving the rest to get their sleep in peace.

Lamps were burning to illuminate the street a bit, but the light wasn't much more than what was necessary to keep people from breaking their necks while stepping off the boardwalk. It was a moonless night with clouds hanging so low that it seemed you could feel them brushing against the top of your head.

Even with so little else going on in the immediate vicinity, the three figures managed to walk toward the hotel without attracting much attention. There were still windows open and the occasional passerby, but not one eye in the vicinity was directed toward the three men.

Part of this was because the three men were dressed in clothes blacker than the night and knew the streets of Origin well enough to avoid every squeaky board. Another part of this came from the fact that, even if locals did spot the black-clad figures, they knew it was best to just look away and forget whatever they might have seen.

The three men stepped up to the hotel, stopping just short of entering the flickering circle of light cast by the lantern on the Broken Banister's porch. Deke stood in the middle of the group, and he looked at each of his partners in turn. Seeing the glance, Marcus and Wilde turned and walked around the hotel in opposite directions.

Once he saw the other two fade into the shadows, Deke stepped onto the porch and opened the front door. He walked into the hotel without a word. His boots hardly even made a sound against the floorboards, and he didn't let go of the door until he'd eased it shut behind him.

Like every other building in town, the Broken Banister held no surprises for Deke. He and his men could have covered every inch of Origin blindfolded, so he instantly knew where to look for the person he was after, the moment he now that the panel in the wall in front of him was shut tightly.

With his senses stretching out for any trace of his prey, Deke walked into the next room and tried the handle on the narrow door leading into the room on the other side of the closed panel. The door was locked, and just before he tried to force it, Deke heard the sound of soft footsteps padding along the floor nearby.

They were a woman's footsteps. He knew that instinctually and turned to follow them to their source.

Wilde stepped around the hotel, keeping his eyes trained on the upper-floor windows. He saw that two of them were illuminated, and there appeared to be someone sitting at the one looking down on the hotel's back lot. Rather than take his chances with Adams, Wilde drew his pistol and held it at his side, with his finger resting on the trigger.

Going up against someone like Clint Adams was both exciting and nerve-wracking at the same time. Killing the

Gunsmith was the same as becoming a god in some circles. Then again, going up against a man like him was also taking a hell of a gamble with your own life. No matter how highly Wilde thought of himself, he knew damn well that those cards were stacked against him.

Then again, with all that Marcus had found out about Adams, some of those odds were evened a bit. It wasn't enough to make Wilde feel as cocky as he normally did, but it was a help all the same.

Wilde froze in his tracks when he heard the window above him being slid open. His nerves tensed and he brought the pistol up, but still managed to keep from making a sound. Someone was looking out through the window, but wasn't leaning out far enough for Wilde to get a look at a face. He didn't get overly anxious, however. His job was to cover that part of the property to cut off any attempt at escape. So long as he remained hidden, he was doing that job well enough.

All the others had to do was flush Adams out and bring him into Wilde's line of fire. From there, Wilde knew he had a good shot at carving out his own bloody niche in the history books.

Marcus walked on the balls of his feet while keeping himself crouched nice and low. As he moved along the side of the hotel, he stepped only where he knew he could do so without drawing attention to himself. In no time at all, he found himself at a spot where two sets of windows came within about three feet of each other.

Gripping onto one window, he placed his foot against the other window and muscled his way up off the ground. Using handholds that could barely accommodate a cat, Marcus made his way to the overhang jutting from the middle of the building. He crouched low and took slow, fluid steps, drawing his pistol before reaching the window where he'd spotted Clint Adams earlier that night.

He couldn't help making a bit of noise as he walked

along the roof, but anything that could be heard could just as easily be written off as the footsteps of a small animal. His gun was in hand and his finger was already tightening around the trigger as Marcus sidled up to the window and eased his way to get a closer peek inside.

By the looks of it, Clint was already in bed, and he might not have even been alone. That didn't make too big of a difference to Marcus. All another person in the room meant to him was that he'd need to use up a few more bullets.

With his free hand, Marcus got a grip on the bottom of the windowpane and prepared to open it. Before doing that, however, he slid along the roof until he was crouched in position. In one explosion of movement, he threw the window open and stuck his hand inside the room.

Sparks lit up the darkness with every shot, filling the room with flickering light. The shots roared and lead filled the air, punching hole after hole through the shape under the blankets.

Hearing the shots, Deke quickened his pace and kicked open the door he was about to sneak through before all hell broke loose. The footsteps he'd been following led to that door, and when he came crashing through, he found a frightened Mexican woman cowering in a corner instead of the clerk he'd been expecting.

"Who are you?" Deke asked, pointing the gun he'd drawn without even having to think about it.

The woman covered her head with both arms and winced at the sound of his voice. She was too scared to speak, but the sight of her alone was enough to get her would-be attacker to leave the room.

Deke rushed up the stairs, not liking where the night was headed. There were times in jobs like that one where a man just knew things weren't headed in the proper direction. People weren't where they were supposed to be and it became clear that someone was one step ahead of the game. Ever since he knew who he was going after, Deke was concerned that Clint Adams would be just the man to turn an easy job on its ear.

Taking the stairs two at a time, he arrived at the top just as the door at the far end of the hall was opened. The man coming from that room was the writer who'd only wanted a few days of quiet, and when he saw Deke lifting his gun, that writer launched himself straight back into his room.

"Jesus Christ," Deke snarled as he stopped himself before firing a round into that writer's hide. Turning toward the room overlooking the street, he made sure to stand away from the opening as he pushed open the door.

Marcus was in there standing over the bed. His gun was in one hand and he held a corner of a charred blanket riddled with bullet holes. Smoke was still drifting up from the barrel of his gun and the room stank of burned black powder.

"You get him?" Deke asked, already fearing the answer.

Pulling off the blanket, Marcus replied, "See for yourself."

Instead of a bloodied body laying under those covers, Deke was shown a set of pillows laying there arranged to roughly resemble a man's form. Feathers still fluttered in the air over the bed, drifting back down onto the messy holes that had been blown through the pillows and mattress.

"Not only am I gonna see that man dead," Deke swore, "but I'm gonna make certain he dies screaming for mercy." His hands gripped the handle of his gun, but the only way to vent his anger was to fire off one more round into the pillow that lay where Clint's head should have been.

THIRTY-ONE

Joan was safe. Clint knew that for a fact because the hotel clerk was in his sight the entire time he made his way back to the courthouse and into the area where prisoners were kept. In his years, Clint had had all too many experiences with gunmen coming after him to let his guard drop so soon after his meeting with Judge Krueger. The menace in the judge's eyes was plain enough to see, and Clint already knew what kind of justice the man dispensed.

If he was wrong, Clint knew there would be no harm done. But Clint knew he wasn't wrong. In fact, he'd wanted to make sure everyone in the hotel was away from there for the night, since that would be the easiest place for an attack to happen. Everyone but the writer staying there had agreed, and they hadn't been able to get ahold of the girl who came in to do the cleaning.

Clint hoped those two were all right, but that was about all he could do at the moment. If those men in black decided to come after him, they wouldn't be deterred for very long by a few strategically placed pillows. There were questions to be answered and one man in town that Clint figured could help him answer them.

The courthouse was locked up for the night, but it

wasn't too hard for Clint to find a way inside. With the judge's main gunmen out for the evening, that only left a few sleepy guards at their posts around the perimeter.

One such guard had been walking along the same patch of ground for so long that he'd practically worn a trench into the dirt. When he turned around, he was surprised to find himself face-to-face with Clint. In fact, both men seemed surprised and weren't able to stop themselves before smacking directly into each other.

"Watch where you're going!" the guard said in a voice that was still a bit shaky from the jolt to his system.

Clint smirked apologetically and took a few steps back. "Sorry about that. Me and my lady friend here were just out for a stroll and—"

Seeing the sheepish look on Clint's face was enough to bring the guard back to his normal posturing. "Just get back to it, whatever you were doing."

"Sure thing. Sorry about that again."

Just as Clint and Joan turned to walk away, the guard stopped and wondered why Clint's face looked so familiar. The shadows were thick and they'd already swallowed up both people, who'd beaten a hasty retreat after the awkward encounter. Shrugging, the guard went back to the chore of trying not to fall asleep.

Heading around the corner, Clint pulled Joan along until he was certain there was plenty of space between them and that guard. They stopped and pressed themselves against a wall.

"Oh my lord," Joan said breathlessly. "Didn't you see that man?"

"Yep," Clint replied. Holding up his hand, he added, "I saw these as well." Dangling from his fingers was the key ring that had been hanging from the guard's belt less than a minute ago. Four keys swung from that ring, and Clint immediately started sifting through them while making his way to one of the courthouse's side doors.

Joan's eyes were wide, and she had to fight to keep herself from laughing out loud. Finally, she calmed herself to talk to Clint in a hurried whisper. "How did you do that? How did you get those?"

"After dealing with too many of the wrong sort of people, you can't help but pick a few things up from them. Besides, that was child's play."

While Clint tried to find the correct key to fit into the lock, Joan replayed the run-in with the guard in her mind. She still couldn't figure out just when Clint had snatched the keys. He must have been real good, real fast, or both. Either way, she was genuinely impressed with Clint, and she couldn't truly say that about many other men.

Clint could feel the way she was looking at him as he worked at the door. Joan's eyes were locked upon him as though he was the only thing in the world at that point in time. When he glanced over to her, he had to admit that there was something different about her.

Before, she'd been somewhat mousy and reserved. Her smile had come easily enough, but it was a warm, friendly type of smile that a kind person would have given to anyone she saw. Her smile was different now. She looked hungrily at him and didn't seem to mind who knew it.

If Clint had been somewhere else, somewhere safer, he would have seen what he could do to make that smile even better. At the moment, however, there were bigger concerns to deal with. As if to make doubly sure that he remained on track, the key Clint had been testing turned in the lock and the door came open.

"Maybe we should find somewhere for you to hide," Clint said. Before he could say another word, he was cut off by a rush of quick, breathy words from Joan's mouth.

"I want to come with you," she blurted. "I can help. At

•

the very least I know I can stay out of the way. You wouldn't want anything to happen to me, would you?"

Clint smiled at her recklessly eager attitude. "Something tells me that you wouldn't stay put for too long no matter where I put you."

Having run her hand briefly along his chest, Joan pulled it back as though she couldn't believe what she'd done. There was a blush in her cheeks that came more from excitement than any sort of shame. "And something tells me that you know a lot about women, Mr. Adams."

"Just promise me that you'll stay close to me and get down if there's any sign of trouble."

"Of course," she said, nodding as though she couldn't actually believe that she was coming along.

Clint would have preferred keeping her a bit safer, but from this point on, he doubted there would be much safety for him or anyone connected to him. At least, not until he got this situation straightened out. The first step in that direction lay down the narrow corridor that Clint found after stepping into the courthouse and locking the door behind him.

THIRTY-TWO

Once he was inside the courthouse, Clint didn't have any trouble finding his way around. He already knew that place better than most people who'd actually had a trial there, and he was only going to know it better. There wasn't much by way of security inside the place until he got closer to the area where prisoners were held between their court dates.

As in most other courthouses, the cells there were only to make things easier on the lawmen who had to take prisoners back and forth. Since there was a proper jailhouse elsewhere in town, the cells in the fancy building were all but vacant. Clint only hoped that the man who'd been taken there earlier was still cooling his heels in one of the cages.

Fortunately, he found another guard standing just inside the narrow doorway leading from the main lobby. Since guards needed something to guard, Clint figured he was in the right place to find his prisoner.

Clint sped down the short hallway and was upon the guard before the man could get a chance to respond to the sound of the door being opened. Using the same speed he'd demonstrated when getting the keys from the man outside, Clint reached out and snatched the guard's gun from his holster.

The lawman spun around and tried to react, but was simply too slow to do anything but gape at the sight in front of him. "Wh . . . what do you want?"

"Just a few moments with your prisoner there," Clint replied. "Oh, and those keys on your belt."

As his eyes darted back and forth between Clint's face and the gun in his hand, the guard fumbled to pull his own set of keys from their spot on his belt.

Clint shook his head as the guard handed the keys over. "First unlock that cell right there," he said, nodding toward one of the empty cages.

The guard did as he was told.

"Get inside," Clint said. Once the guard did that, Clint shut the door and stepped back. "Lock it and toss the keys out when you're through."

Although it took a few moments, the guard eventually resigned himself to his fate and obeyed Clint's orders. After tossing the keys out, he skulked away from the bars and nearly tripped backward over the cot at the back of the cell.

"What now?" the guard asked.

"Now you sit and keep quiet," Clint said. "I need to have a talk with this fellow right here."

Deciding it was best to hold his tongue rather than upset the man holding all the cards, the guard kept to his little corner of the cell without one more protest.

Sticking the guard's pistol under his gunbelt, Clint shifted his focus over to the only other cell in the small room that was occupied. Although not half as worked up as he'd been when he was dragged from the courtroom not too long ago, the man was undoubtedly the person Clint wanted to see.

He was a stout figure with bushy hair and a messy beard. Although he'd been watching everything that had happened, he still had yet to move from the spot where he was slouched upon his own cot. His arms were wrapped around his knees, pulling himself up into an uncomfortable ball.

"Howdy," Clint said.

The other man's reaction was hardly noticeable. He finally gave a nod in return, but it was barely enough to move his hairy head.

"I saw you coming out of the—"

"Yeah," the man in the cell interrupted. "I remember you."

"Good," Clint said, stepping forward so he could extend an open hand through the bars. "My name's Clint Adams."

The man in the cell paused, turned to look at the humiliated guard and then turned back to Clint. He finally did get up so he could shake Clint's hand. "Mick Shoemaker. I hope you didn't go through all this trouble to break me out of here. It'd just get us both killed."

"Actually, I wanted to have a word with you before I did anything else."

"What about?"

"Judge Krueger."

The mention of that name was enough to stoke Mick's fire back to its former intensity. After pulling a breath into his lungs, he reared up and took hold of the bars with both hands. As he spoke, he tightened his grasp around the iron bars as if he was wringing someone's neck.

"That bastard ain't hardly a judge," Mick said. "He's more of an animal than anything else. How that animal got to wear those judge's robes isn't just a mystery, but it's a damn shame as well."

Clint nodded. "I've been thinking the same thing. How much do you know about him?"

Suddenly, Mick's eyes narrowed and he stopped himself before saying what he was going to say. "Why do you want to know, exactly?"

"Because I stumbled upon some of the judge's handiwork and it made my stomach turn."

"What're you talking about?"

Clint went on to tell Mick a brief rundown of what had brought him to the point of breaking into a courthouse just so he could get to the holding cells. As Mick listened, he did so without much of a change of expression. He merely nodded and took it all in. Every so often, his hands would wring the bars a bit more. Finally, once Clint was done, Mick let go of the bars and smirked.

"You got some sand, mister," Mick said. "Most folks tend to either pay tribute to the judge or turn tail and run when they see half of what you did."

"So this isn't the first time Krueger's hung someone like that?"

"Not hardly."

"How many have there been?"

"I doubt if anyone but him could answer that. I know he keeps track of all the messages he sends. Him and those Four Horsemen of his. I'm the next one to get one of them notes nailed to my chest."

"Why?" Clint asked. "What did you do?"

"I made it clear that I would do my best to make sure he doesn't take over this whole damn county."

THIRTY-THREE

This time, Clint was the one wearing the odd look on his face, and it was plain enough for everyone to see. Mick raised his eyebrows and nodded just to let Clint know that whatever he was thinking, things were probably worse.

"Yeah," Mick said. "It's that bad."

"How would Judge Krueger be able to take over a county?" Clint asked.

"He's got his finger in a whole lot of pies, and it all started out with him doing what he does best."

"And what's that?"

"Hanging folks."

"So he's a hanging judge," Clint said. "There's plenty of them around. That doesn't give Krueger any special brand of power."

"That all depends on who you hang." Mick leaned against the bars and kept his back to the guard in the next cell. "You dig deep enough into any man's past or present and you can always find something bad. You put the right spin on things in a courtroom and you can make any man sound guilty.

"What Krueger does is put those services up for hire. That way, he can take a fee from some politician or land baron and all he has to do is make sure whoever is on trial gets railroaded all the way to a noose."

Clint scowled and shook his head. "That's nothing too new either. There's crooked judges in every state."

"Maybe, but Krueger only got started that way. He's branched out plenty since then. He's got aspirations."

"Like what? Politics?"

"Nah. He works behind the politicians. He gets in their good graces and becomes a valuable partner so it don't even matter who's in office. They'll all want him on their side. Think about it. Anyone who knows how to approach Krueger can pay to have their enemies publicly put through hell in a trial, their name dragged through the mud, and then have them killed.

"While doing dirty business like that, he's gotten to know plenty of valuable information. He don't kill every man he's paid to. Some of them know enough to bargain for their lives, and some of them even have enough to save their own skin."

"So Krueger takes money from the rich targets?" Clint asked.

Mick shook his head. "He takes information. He digs up dirt, gets secrets and finds out plans other men have made so he can act on them himself. And if anyone gets in his way, they wind up being put on trial and hung for thieving or the murder of some other poor bastard Krueger's men shot down just to supply a body."

"The Four Horsemen," Clint stated, repeating the term he'd heard earlier.

"Yeah. That's what they're called because everyone around here knows that they're like the coming of the apocalypse to anyone they're after. There've been plenty of them throughout the years, but no more than four at a time and they've always been led by Deke Gray."

Clint didn't need to ask about Deke. He could picture the cold, piercing eyes and the lean face covered by a bushy mustache. One look into those eyes was enough to tell him that they belonged to a seasoned killer and not just some gunhand.

"So Krueger has a nice little operation running," Clint said. "How does he go from there to taking over an entire county?"

"It started small enough. Soon, Krueger started going after men on his own rather than taking fees to kill other people's enemies. He started going after the land barons and politicians. They didn't think much of him at first, until the first one wound up in his courtroom.

"Public outcry was so bad that a mob formed to try and cut the man down as he swung from the noose. But them Horsemen pulled their guns and went to work on anyone they could hit." Mick paused and got a look in his eye as though he was reliving a bad dream. "It didn't matter to Deke. Didn't matter to any of them. Women, old-timers, even a few kids caught some lead that day. Ever since then, Krueger hung his victims out where others could see them and away from a crowd. That's when he started putting them notes on them. I guess he figured he'd make it work for him."

Shaking his head to clear out the screams that still echoed in his mind, Mick fixed his eyes back onto Clint. "Anyway, after that, Krueger became something of a legend around here. Kind of like a monster that everyone believes in but doesn't want to mention. I met up with someone who not only knew more about him than me but who was willing to do something to put Krueger down for good. That is, until Krueger got his hands on him."

"Who are you talking about?" Clint asked.

"I guess it don't matter much now since he's dead. Man's name was Jeremiah Ambrose."

Clint nodded when he heard the name that he'd purposely kept out of the account he'd told to Mick. "You mean One-Thumb?"

"You know him?"

"Sure do. He's the hanged man I found on my way into Trickle Creek."

"Jesus! So he's alive?"

Clint nodded. "As far as I know. He went missing before I could check on him again. What's he got to do with all of this?"

"Jeremiah owns some land that Krueger intended to offer to the railroads in exchange for some big favors. There's a few ranchers out for the same property as well, so he meant to do some big-time dealing. Jeremiah wouldn't sell, and somewhere along the line he overheard enough to tell him that Krueger was the one pulling the strings in this deal.

"It goes one deal at a time," Mick explained. "Just follow the evidence and you can see it for yourself. Bit by bit, Krueger gets a little more power, until he's at the point he's at now where he can influence the decisions that make fortunes and shape policy. Power like that is only held in a few hands and Krueger is a few steps away from being one of them."

"And you wound up in here because you can prove all this?" Clint asked.

"Actually, I wound up in here because of the stink you raised. Otherwise, I would have been swinging from my own tree out in the middle of nowhere by now. But yeah, I can prove it. All the proof you need is in a set of leather books up in Krueger's office. That's where he keeps records of his trials and executions so he can look good to any other legal types that come along to question him."

As he listened to Mick speak, Clint pictured the very books that he was talking about. In fact, he could still see Judge Krueger standing there in his office with his hand on one of those volumes.

"Them books are in code, though," Mick added. "And

that's where ol' One-Thumb really became a pain in the ass to Krueger."

"He figured out the code?"

"Yep, but he don't even realize it. One-Thumb just heard some strange talk and just happened to remember every bit of it. I figured it out after talking to him and was able to get a look at them books. That's how I wound up on trial. Them books can put Krueger in his place."

Clint thought that over and didn't come away from it nearly as enthused as Mick. If Judge Krueger had half the power Mick was describing, he was too smart to let his entire future rest on a set of coded record books.

"So are you gonna let me out of here?" Mick asked.

After taking a moment to decide what to do, Clint shook his head. "Nope. I didn't come here to break you out." Turning his gaze toward the locked-up guard, Clint said, "And don't worry. I didn't forget about you."

THIRTY-FOUR

It didn't take long for Deke to make his way back to the courthouse. His other two men were scouring the rest of the town, looking for any trace of Clint Adams or anyone else who they didn't find in that hotel. He knew that if he didn't find Adams right away, one of those others would have a good idea of where to look next.

But Deke reserved the right to cover the courthouse himself. After all, he figured that was the best bet of where Adams might be since he'd already showed up there enough times already. Unlike the other men in black, Deke was able to think ahead and put an entire picture together without needing someone else to trace the pattern for him.

He approached the courthouse from the side, knowing better than to strut right into the open where someone might be looking for him. Even though he could only make out a single shape in the shadows surrounding the massive building, he already saw enough to let him know something wasn't right.

First of all, there was only one man on patrol that he could see. One of the guards was either missing, laying low or preoccupied. Whichever it turned out to be would only serve to prove Deke's initial suspicions correct. He strode right up to the guard he could see and brushed aside the man's first attempts at striking up a conversation.

"Where's the other one?" Deke asked brusquely.

For a moment, the guard looked around as if he was trying to figure out what Deke might be talking about.

Deke responded to that by backhanding the guard across the face hard enough to rattle him in his boots. "Don't pretend like you don't know what I mean. Where's the other man that's supposed to be walking the perimeter?"

"He's inside."

"Why's he inside?"

"Because someone came by and he thinks he might have taken his keys."

Clenching his fist, Deke had to struggle to keep from knocking the guard clean off his feet. Instead, Deke grabbed hold of the guard's shirt and pulled him along behind him as he went to the side entrance. "See this door?" he asked, shoving the guard forward as if he was shoving a dog's nose into a pile of shit. "Keep an eye on this one and the front one and start shooting at anyone who isn't me that comes out of there."

"Both doors? I can't—"

"I don't care if you need to run back and forth like your tail's on fire. If it'll help, I'll set your ass on fire personally."

Nodding vigorously, the guard said, "I can do it. But what if I see—"

"If it ain't me that comes out of that building, I want you to shoot them. That includes that dumb shit partner of yours. Shooting him before I get to him would only be doing that asshole a favor."

With that, Deke let go of the guard and tried the side door. It was locked, so he used his own set of keys to get inside without making so much as a hint of noise along the way. The courthouse was dark and mostly quiet. It would have been completely quiet if not for the tapping of foot-steps coming from the main entrance area.

Deke walked on the balls of his feet and had his pistol drawn before he reached the end of his short hallway. The footsteps were getting closer, and when they were close enough, Deke reached out to grab hold of the person making them.

There was hardly any struggle from the man Deke grabbed. The guy was just too surprised to do much of anything as he was dragged into the hallway by a hand that reached out from the depths of a shadow.

Deke found himself staring into the vaguely familiar face of the guard whose proper place was outside the building.

"J-Jesus, Deke. You scared the . . . sh-shit out of me," the guard stammered.

"Where'd he go?" was all Deke needed to ask.

"I'm not sure, but he's not upstairs, because I—"

"You checked upstairs first?"

"Y-yeah. The judge's chambers."

Nodding, Deke pushed the guard aside. "You still have your gun? Or did you lose that, too?"

"I've still got it."

"Then go outside and do your job. You see anyone else come out of here that ain't me, you shoot them. Got it?"

The guard looked a little confused, but nodded and agreed just to keep in Deke's good graces. He then rushed down the hall and left through the same door that Deke had just used to come in.

Deke stood and waited to see if he was going to hear a shot from the other guard, but he got only silence. That didn't matter to him, though. There was going to be plenty of shooting before too long.

THIRTY-FIVE

Deke was wound up so tightly that he was ready to shoot at any trace of movement he saw or heard. His reflexes snapped his aim toward each and every scraping or creak he came across, but those same reflexes kept him from pulling his trigger before wasting a shot.

The first place he went was to the holding cells in the bowels of the courthouse. Since Adams seemed to be so interested in the prisoner being held there, he'd probably set up the entire distraction at the hotel to buy him time to meet with him. Deke didn't much care about Adams's reasons. All he wanted was to get his sights on him.

Just once.

That was all he'd need.

There was another guard missing. Deke noticed that the moment he opened the narrow door that led away from the main room of the courthouse. There should have been a guard patrolling that little hallway, but instead there was nothing. Gritting his teeth, Deke knew he was close to Adams. He could feel it. Keeping his back to the wall, Deke walked in a sidestep down the hall with his gun held ready at his hip.

Finally, he stepped into the room with the cells and prepared to put an end to the days of the Gunsmith.

There was an extra person in the cells and it only took a fraction of a second for Deke to pick out which of those men was the prisoner that belonged there. He set his sights on the other man in that room and almost pulled his trigger out of sheer frustration.

"What the hell?" Deke snarled at the guard who sat sheepishly in his own cell. "Start explaining or I'll empty your guts onto that cot."

The guard was trembling, holding his hands up in front of him as though they would be enough to stop a bullet. "He's been here and gone already. There wasn't anything I could do."

"Yeah," Mick said from his own cell. "He knows you mean to kill me without good reason."

Deke shifted his eyes over to Mick. "I don't need good reason, but the judge has plenty of them. Besides, you were found guilty."

"Yeah, by the finest jury money could buy."

"Ain't nobody bought them. Of course, nobody consulted them either. You sealed your fate when you decided to take on the wrong man. You shoulda taken Judge Krueger's offer when you had the chance."

"Does it still stand?" Mick asked sarcastically.

A smile crept onto Deke's face, but it looked like something closer to a lizard slithering onto the sunny side of a rock. His laugh was a grumble at the back of his throat, and he was still laughing as he reached out to grab hold of Mick's shirt and pull him face-first into the bars.

"You're damn lucky to be standing yourself," Deke snarled. "And I might just save us some rope by killing you right here and now if you don't answer everything I ask you. Is that clear?"

Blood trickled from one of Mick's nostrils as well as from one side of his mouth. Even if his hands weren't pinned against the bars, however, he still wouldn't have reached up to wipe the blood away. Instead, he just nodded.

Deke nodded as well. "Good," he said. "Now, tell me something. Did you get any unexpected visitors tonight?"

"Y-yeah. I did."

After giving a brief description of Clint, Deke asked, "Was that the man who came to see you?"

"Yeah."

"What did you tell him?"

"I told him that I wasn't supposed to be locked up here. I also told him the only reason I was locked up was because I was against Judge Krueger becoming the man in charge of this whole county."

Hearing this, Deke only nodded some more. The smile was still crawling around beneath his thick mustache. "This county? He'll be in charge of the entire state before too long."

"Just because of all the crooked politicians that are kissing his ass."

"Yeah, and you could have been along for the ride. Instead, you decided to be an asshole and try to mess things up. Well, I got some news for you. There ain't anything else you can do about Judge Krueger. Nobody can help you. Not even Clint Adams. Your only way out now is to tell us where we might be able to find that cock-sucking farmer Ambrose. You think you can manage that?"

Deke's words were obviously having an effect on Mick. They caused him to squirm against the bars as a sheet of sweat broke out from his forehead and ran down his face. But he held his ground all the same. "After what you fellas did to him, I wouldn't be surprised if Ambrose never shows his face again. He's probably been running so hard that he doesn't even know where he is."

Staring into the man's eyes, Deke pulled in a breath and weighed his options. Finally, he stepped back, but not before pulling on Mick one last time to smack him against the bars. "Fine. Have it your way," Deke said. "The next time I see you, we'll drag you out to a tree and hang you from it. Or maybe I'll have one of the others stop by with your son or sister. Maybe you'll feel more like talking once you see them get taken apart for a while."

"You son of a bitch!"

But Deke had already turned around and was headed out of the holding area. He didn't pay any mind to the insults Mick spat at him. He didn't even seem to hear the guard who yelled out at him.

"Hey!" the guard shouted. "What about me?"

"You're not much use doing your job," Deke said just before stepping through the door. "So take a rest for a while. Those cots look real comfortable."

The guard squirmed as he'd been doing the entire time Deke was in the room. Even after the sound of the door closing came through the room, followed by the muted clomp of footsteps, the guard kept on squirming. He hopped up off the cot once Deke was long gone.

As soon as the guard was off the cot, the entire wooden frame came up off the ground to reveal the spot where Clint had been laying with his back and heels against the wall. The gun he'd been pointing at the guard through the cot was still in hand and remained fixed upon its target.

"You hear all that?" Mick asked while angrily swiping at the blood and sweat running down his face.

"I did," Clint replied while dusting off the front of his shirt. "Every word of it."

"And what do you think? You think you can let me out of here now?"

"Maybe, but only on one condition."

His bruises forgotten, Mick scrambled right back up to the bars. "Anything. Just name it."

"You need to stick with me, or somewhere I can find

you. If I find out that you belong in a cell, for any reason whatsoever, that's right where you'll be headed."

"Where are you going?" Mick shouted as Clint turned his back on the cells and started heading toward the only door out.

"There's just a few more things I need to do here and I'll be back for you."

As he walked toward the door, Clint noticed something peculiar about the narrow hallway. Hardly any of the light from the lanterns near the holding cells reached that far, but there seemed to be something odd about the shadows around the door.

Then Clint realized that there were no shadows around the door. There was something blocking the door altogether, and by the time Clint realized that it was a man standing in the shadows, it was too late.

A pistol came swinging from the darkness and caught Clint square on the temple so fast that he didn't even see what had hit him. He felt it, though. He felt it for the couple of seconds before losing consciousness.

THIRTY-SIX

Clint's entire world was brought down to the throbbing pain filling his skull. That pounding was like a hammer slamming against the inside of his head and sending his blood in powerful bursts through his veins. The ground seemed to be sliding beneath him, making Clint feel like he was sliding off the side of the world.

He could hear voices, but not well enough to make out any words. He knew there were others around him, but had no idea how many or where they were. For that matter, he didn't even know where he was until he heard a familiar kind of sound.

The sound wasn't anything in particular, but more of a shading to the words that struck a chord in Clint's mind. It was an echoing at the end of every word, combined with a scraping of boots against stone.

That was it.

In that instant, Clint knew exactly what he was hearing and where he was.

He was hearing the echo of voices within a huge, empty room and the scraping was his own boots being dragged against a hard, polished surface. Clint had heard that sound plenty of times, whenever anyone took a step inside the main room of the courthouse. That echo had accompanied every word spoken in that same room.

With that realization dawning on him, Clint opened his eyes and prepared himself to take a swing at the first person he saw.

"He's starting to kick," came a vaguely familiar voice. "I think he's waking up."

Deke's was the first face Clint saw, but he was unable to do anything since his hands were being held in iron grips.

"You're a tough one," Deke said. "I'll bet you last a good long time before you die. I guess we'll just have to see for ourselves."

The words came like whispers from a grave and were punctuated by another blow from the handle of Deke's gun. This time, however, Clint was able to twist himself around so most of the blow was caught by his shoulder and part of his neck. It didn't feel good, but at least it didn't threaten to knock him out completely.

Clint not only guessed that the men holding his wrists would tighten their grip, he counted on it. If they didn't, he wouldn't be able to use them so well to his own advantage. Pulling against the hands holding his wrists, Clint brought his lower body up and his legs straight up off the floor.

Clint felt one leg graze against something solid, but his other leg came up against two solid objects. Those two objects just happened to be Deke's legs, and the next solid thing Clint's leg slammed against was Deke's crotch.

Deke let out a choking, gurgling sound as he crumpled over with pain. With the pressure still fierce around his wrists, Clint dropped both feet to the ground and pushed himself back in the opposite direction of that pressure. Between Clint's own strength and his sudden change in direction, he was able to get one arm free.

Rather than try to pull against the other man that still had ahold of one of his arms, Clint reached over with his free hand to take hold of his remaining captor's arm to use it as an anchor to pull himself up. It was an awkward move at best, but it served its purpose well enough. In the space of a couple seconds, Clint was on his feet and facing the youngest of the Four Horsemen.

Hanging on as if he was trying to keep hold of a bucking bronco, Wilde planted his feet and tightened his grip around Clint's wrist. He could see Marcus on the other side of Clint, struggling to regain his balance after being pushed aside.

Although Clint had a solid hold on both of Wilde's hands, it had taken both of his own hands to do it. That didn't leave him much choice of weapons to use against the younger man, so Clint lashed out with the first one that came to mind. Without giving himself time to think better of the plan, Clint snapped his head forward and slammed his forehead against the bridge of Wilde's nose. Clint was already groggy enough to shake off the impact, but Wilde wasn't so lucky.

The younger man couldn't let go of Clint fast enough as he staggered back and pressed both hands flat against his face. Venomous curses spewed from between his fingers, almost as much as the blood did, as Wilde reeled back from the jarring impact.

Clint swung around, leading with his fist. His knuckles caught Marcus in the chest before Clint got a good look at his target. Although the punch didn't do much by way of damage, it stopped Marcus just long enough for Clint to get a better look and follow up with another swing. This time, Clint's fist pounded squarely into the side of Marcus's jaw, spinning the man around on the balls of his feet.

All the while, Deke had been watching the fight and keeping himself far enough from it to avoid catching a stray punch. The pain of Clint's kick still brought the bile up from his gullet, but he'd managed to channel that pain into fuel for the rage inside of him.

Once Marcus had been knocked back, Deke was

granted the very thing he'd been waiting for while trying to keep himself from puking up his dinner: a clean shot.

Deke's hand dropped to the holster at his side and was instantly filled with iron. In the next moment, he took aim.

Clint was still trying to shake the cobwebs from his skull when he found himself staring down the barrel of Deke's gun. That moment froze in time for both of them. Deke was savoring the moment before his final kill, and Clint was praying to God that the Colt was still in its holster.

When that moment ticked by, Clint's hand flashed to his holster just as Deke squeezed his trigger.

The Colt was gone.

Deke's shot blasted through the air.

Clint's world once again went black.

THIRTY-SEVEN

Sometimes, Clint thought about what it would be like to die. He'd seen plenty of men meet their end, and had sent more that his fair share of them to their maker. But as for himself, Clint preferred not to give the matter too much thought. He figured he'd find out for himself soon enough.

Every so often, though, he couldn't help but let the subject cross his mind. Now was one of those times, simply because he was starting to think that he was actually at the end of his time on God's green earth.

Then the pain set in.

When the first wave of agony rolled through him, Clint knew damn well that he wasn't dead. Dead men didn't feel a pain that caused every one of their joints to throb. They either felt nothing at all, pure bliss or eternal hellfire. It depended on which belief a man subscribed to, but none of them mentioned a thing about headaches and double knots in the stomach.

With such things still coursing through his mind, Clint tried to move, and felt the pain spike even higher. His first impulse was to suck in a breath, which felt painful and yet awfully good at the same time.

"I'm not dead," Clint wheezed, unsure as to whether or

not he'd actually spoken the words out loud.

"No," came the reply through all the fog in Clint's brain. "You're not."

Clint blinked a few times, tried to get up and then felt himself get pushed right back down again. After a few more steadying breaths, he started to see some things come into focus. The sights were a long ways from being clear, but he recognized enough to put a name to the face that was smiling down at him.

"You came awfully close," Joan said. "But you're not dead yet."

Although the effort of breathing felt like he was driving a stake through his own chest, Clint kept it up. Every bit of air in his lungs awakened him even more. But more than that, it was another step back from the brink.

"What happened?" he asked weakly. "Where am I?"

Joan had a rag in her hands and was wringing water from it into a bowl next to where Clint was laying. "You're safe. We both are. My boss rents out cabins all over town. We're at one that is too run-down to be rented anymore. It's not in the books and nobody else remembers it's even here. When I told him that you meant to stand against Judge Krueger, he insisted we stay here until you were feeling better."

As he took in more breaths, Clint also took in more of his surroundings. From what he could see, Joan was telling the truth about where they were. The walls around him were pieced together from crooked, rotten planks. The air stank of mold, and dirt hung like a veil in the air, causing each ray of sunlight to show like it had been painted in gold.

He scraped his fingers against the floor beneath him and discovered he was laying on a threadbare blanket on top of more rotten planks. Outside, the occasional sound could be heard, but far off in the distance.

"Wait a second," he said to himself in a grumbling

voice. "Daylight?" Looking up to Joan, Clint asked, "What time is it? How long have I been here?"

She patted him on the head before dabbing the wet cloth against his skin. "It's about three o'clock. Don't worry, though. You can rest all day long if you need to."

"So I've been here about half a day?"

"Well, it's actually more like two and a half days."

THIRTY-EIGHT

"What?" The shock Clint felt caused him to sit straight up and take a better look around for himself. Actually, he tried to sit up, but only wound up getting about halfway before the pain in his chest and torso sent him down faster than a boot to the chin.

Joan placed her hand flat against his chest and didn't have to push too hard to keep him down. "You need to rest. Don't try to get up or do anything else."

Clint struggled against her for another second or two, which was just the amount of time he needed to know that he should stop. It wasn't that he couldn't break away from her, but Clint could tell he wouldn't be able to do much of anything once he was free. So rather than waste any more energy, he settled back and caught his breath.

"What happened at the courthouse?" he asked.

"What do you remember?"

"I remember talking to Mick and then getting knocked in the head. I woke up and tussled some more and then I was . . ." Before he could finish his sentence, Clint's thoughts were overwhelmed by the memory of that last gunshot from Deke's gun. He could still feel the pain that shot had caused, but not much else after that.

"You were shot," Joan said. "And you would have been killed if not for the good Lord."

"It had to have been something else," Clint said after touching his hand to his chest and feeling the pain that came from the slightest tap of his fingers. "That bullet should have done me in."

In response to that, Joan reached to a small table and held something out for Clint to see. The heavy metal cross looked just as rough as when One-Thumb's wife had given it to him, only now one of the arms was bent almost ninety degrees from where it should have been. There was a dent near the center of the cross which looked like someone had poked their finger nearly through the thick metal.

Seeing that, Clint reached down to pull open his shirt and get a look at his chest. Although he couldn't see the entire wound from his vantage point, he could see enough of the dark blue-and-black bruise to know it was in the shape of that same, rusty cross.

"Good Lord, indeed," Clint said after a low whistle. "I guess I used up my portion of luck for the next year or two."

Nodding, Joan said, "Either that, or someone's looking out for you."

"It feels like I might have cracked a rib or two, but it sure beats the alternative."

"There wasn't much bleeding, but it looked a lot worse when I found you. I thought you were dead for sure." Joan left Clint's sight for a moment to get some more water.

Following her with his eyes gave Clint the opportunity to get a better look at the cabin. What little furniture it had was barricading the door. Whatever blankets Clint wasn't using were hanging over the windows to cut them off from the outside world.

Joan came back with a dented tin cup full of water. After helping Clint sit up, she handed him the cup. "Is that all you remember from that night?"

"I did tell you to find somewhere safe to hide while I waited in that cell," Clint recalled. "It turned out we had even less time than I figured."

"Well, I found a spot just in time. It was a broom closet that was full of cobwebs, but it served its purpose just fine. I heard the first scuffle, but couldn't get out since all those gunmen started coming in. After the second fight, I waited until it was clear before coming out." Lowering her eyes, she added, "I was too scared to do much else. I'm sorry."

"There wasn't anything you could have done. That is," Clint added with a smirk, "unless you're a deadly gunhand and you never told me."

"No. Nothing of the sort."

"Then you did the right thing. If they'd gotten ahold of you, it would have only made matters worse. So how did I get from there to here, anyway?"

"Like I said, I came out from hiding once the noise stopped, and I found you laying on the floor. I wasn't the only one coming out for a look, because those gunmen were gone as well. Either that, or they just left you for dead.

"You were covered in blood, but still breathing, so I took a look at you and saw that you weren't really shot after all. While I was doing that, you came around and started trying to move. I helped you up and got you out of there so we could find some help."

While he listened to her, Clint tried to remember any of what she was describing. To him, it was like trying to remember a dream from ten years ago. Some of it rang true, but not even half of it. Mostly, there were just bits and pieces that didn't make one lick of sense.

"The doctor took a look at you and said you should be all right after getting some bed rest."

"Wait a minute," Clint interrupted. "I went to a doctor?"

Joan nodded. "You were passing in and out the whole time. At least you could walk; otherwise I wouldn't have been able to get you out of the courthouse. Once you got here, you laid down on the floor and have been out since. I tried to get you onto the bed, but you're just too heavy."

Straining his neck to get a look at the space behind him, Clint did spot a rickety bed not too far away. The thing was so old and worn, however, that it didn't look too much better than the spot he'd picked out on the floor.

"Where's my gun?" Clint asked.

"I don't know. It was all I could do to get you out of there. Those men must have taken it from you."

Clint nodded. The truth was that he hadn't really expected to come out of that courthouse with his life and gun. As it stood, he knew he'd gotten a pretty good deal.

Even though he dreaded the answer he might get, Clint still had to ask the question. "What about Mick?"

"Oh, I set him loose. He even helped me get you out once I used the keys you'd stolen to unlock his cell."

Clint was surprised by the news and felt a surge of hope give him some extra strength. "Where is he now?"

"He said he wanted to try and find that friend of his, One-Thumb."

Suddenly, Clint felt his strength leaving him. As he laid down and closed his eyes, he realized things weren't quite as bad as he'd thought they would be. They weren't exactly good, but sometimes a man had to take whatever he could get.

THIRTY-NINE

When Clint awoke, the light coming through the slats of the wall was weaker than before and slanting at a different angle. Although his first instinct was that he'd only been asleep for a little while, he wasn't about to put all his faith in his own sense of time just yet.

He straightened up and pulled in a slow breath. It felt good to move a bit more on his own steam, but those movements were still a painful experience. Clasping a hand to his chest made it easier to get up, but he soon realized that the near miss from that bullet wasn't his only concern. His sense of balance was off, making every step wobbly, and his vision was still a bit on the cloudy side.

As far as he could tell, Joan wasn't in the cabin. That was probably for the best, since she would have surely tried to stop him from walking around the dirty, cluttered space. Clint found a chipped shaving mirror hanging from a nail in one wall and picked it up to get a look at himself.

"Jesus," he whispered once he did. Clint had caught plenty of punches in his life and had dealt out plenty more, but he must have caught about double the amount he remembered from Deke.

His face was swollen like an overripe melon and his

157

eyes were hardly even halfway open. There were welts on his cheeks and a few knots on his forehead, topped off by nasty looking gashes that would have been downright scary if they hadn't been cleaned up. Seeing himself now, Clint truly realized what had been the cause of his forced nap over the last couple of days.

Deke and his boys might as well have danced on his skull. That would also have explained why Clint was still a bit dizzy after only having stood up for a few minutes. Even so, he still wanted to get out of the cabin and get back to work. Just thinking about Deke and Judge Krueger made his blood boil. When he heard the door coming open, Clint turned around and reflexively grabbed for the gun that wasn't there.

"It's only me," Joan said. "I had to get some food. It took a while because I needed to stay out of sight, but there's plenty of folks around here who wanted to help once they knew I was taking care of you."

Clint made his way over to the rickety bed and set himself down. The frame creaked beneath his weight and started to shift in a way that made Clint stand right back up again.

Joan set down what she'd been carrying and made sure the door was shut and locked up tight. From there, she rushed over to give Clint a steadying hand. "Here," she said. "Why don't you try the chair? It'll probably hold you a bit better."

"Thanks," Clint said as he placed his arm over Joan's shoulders and let her help him over to the chair. Sure enough, the chair held up and Clint allowed himself to relax. "It feels good to be off my back."

"I know what can make you feel even better."

For a moment, Clint wondered what Joan had in mind. He watched her turn and bend to pick up the packages she'd set down moments ago. He couldn't help but notice the smooth line of her backside shifting beneath the thin layers of her skirts. Her hips were trim and rounded just enough. When she turned, her pert breasts swung slightly beneath her blouse.

"Here's the food I brought," she said, proudly handing over a plate covered by a napkin. Pulling off the napkin, she announced, "Baked chicken, gravy and peas. There's some mashed potatoes as well and even some pie."

"That's a lot of food, but I think I can handle it. I hope it wasn't too much trouble."

She shrugged. "Not hardly. After what Judge Krueger's been putting this town through, folks around here already think of you as a hero. Word's gotten around about how you freed Mick and killed one of those horrible gunmen. After all that, you could probably become mayor of Ori gin."

"I'd have to get through Judge Krueger first," Clint pointed out, more to himself than her.

Joan nodded as a shadow fell over her face. "I suppose so. He's been laying low since what happened. Canceled all his trials but one. I think he's scared." Suddenly, the light came back to her face. "You really were hungry."

Clint had already devoured almost half his food. Gravy clung to the stubble on his face, and he was about to shovel some potatoes into his mouth, when he gave her a nod and smile. He cleaned off his plate in minutes and handed it over to Joan.

She'd watched him eat, and filled his water cup a few times, but hadn't said much of anything else. When she saw he was finished, she took the plate from him and went over to fetch the washcloth she'd been using to dab the blood from his face.

"You're looking better," she said, moving up close to him so she could get a look at his wounds.

The light from outside had faded away to nothing by this time. Under normal circumstances, they would have lit one of the lanterns laying about, but these circumstances were far from normal. Joan was holding up well, but was still too nervous to draw any undue attention, and Clint simply knew better.

"It's amazing what a good meal can do for a man," Clint said. "I feel like I could ride out of here tonight."

"You're not going anywhere tonight, Clint. You can barely walk."

"Well, I can't exactly stay around here for too much longer. When is the trial Krueger scheduled?"

"The day after tomorrow. You think you can stay put until then?"

Clint started to get up, but felt the room teeter slightly beneath him. "I probably could use a bit more rest."

Approaching even closer to him, Joan wiped away something from Clint's face. She was close enough for him to smell her and close enough for wisps of her light brown hair to brush against his face. "You're a mess, Clint," she said while dabbing at some of the gravy he'd spilled.

After setting down his plate and cup, Clint reached out to take hold of her hips with both hands. He pulled Joan closer to him until she was straddling his lap. "Even though I'm not all the way back yet, I am feeling a lot better."

FORTY

Joan allowed herself to be pulled closer and finally lowered herself down onto his lap. "You must be feeling better." She could feel his erection through his pants and rubbed herself against him until he was even harder. "Yes," she whispered. "You sure are feeling pretty good from here."

Moving his hands up and down her sides, Clint let his palms get higher and lower with every pass. As Joan settled down on top of him, he slid his hands up until he was almost cupping her breasts. From there, he went down again until his fingers grazed her inner thigh.

Joan let out a contented sigh as she moved in time to his hands. When he ran them up over her body once more, she lifted herself up slightly in anticipation. Her breath came out in a louder gasp when she felt Clint's hands fully grasp her breasts. His hands were strong without being rough. His thumbs moved in just the right way to make her little nipples stand erect beneath her blouse.

Just before Joan caught her breath, she felt his hands moving again. This time, they traveled down to her hips, sliding over them and onto her thighs, without stopping until they'd reached her knees. He stayed there for less than a second before moving up and in to caress her inner thigh.

Although Joan wanted to keep mirroring his movements, she stopped short when she felt Clint's fingers between her legs. If she moved so much as an inch, she might
have lost the tingling sensation he was giving her. So, with
her eyes clenched tightly shut, she stayed where she was as
Clint sent chills through her entire body.

Clint could feel the heat coming from Joan's body. It
got even hotter as he started massaging the spot between
her legs. She began swaying slightly, and Clint had to sup-
port her with one hand while the other remained busy.

The only time he paused was to reach down and slip his
hand under her skirts. She was wearing a few layers of
flimsy cotton, which Clint reached past until he got back to
the spot he'd been before. All it took was a little tug for him
to get past Joan's undergarments and then his fingers were
rubbing against the soft, downy hair between her legs.

Her pussy was soft, warm and became wetter with every
pass of his hand. Clint massaged her until he could feel her
straining for breath, and only then did he slip one finger
gently inside of her.

Joan's eyes snapped open and she looked down at him
as though she'd been caught doing something bad. The
pleasure quickly overwhelmed her, sweeping away what
little nervousness remained. In moments, she was grasping
onto Clint's shoulders and arching her back as she felt his
fingers slide in and out of her.

Just when she thought the pleasure had reached its highest point, she felt his thumb start brushing against her clitoris. Once that started, she was the one who had a hard
time remembering where she was. The cabin as well as the
rest of the world became a swirl of passion, leaving only
her and Clint behind.

She lost what little hesitation she had and gave herself
entirely over to him, spreading her legs and grinding against
his hand. Her pussy was becoming wetter by the moment,

and when Clint found that single, perfect spot on her, Joan placed her hand upon his to keep him from moving.

Clint followed her lead perfectly, keeping his fingers placed just so while he massaged that spot gently. Soon, her body was trembling and her breath was coming in a quickening pace. Her eyes clenched shut tightly and her pussy tightened around his fingers.

Her orgasm swept through her like a storm, leaving her breathless and weak for a moment. That moment passed, however. When she opened her eyes to look at him again, there was no disguising the hunger there. Her breasts were heaving with every breath, and it seemed as though she would have ripped her own clothes off if Clint wasn't already doing just that.

Clint was getting harder just watching the look on Joan's face. The motion of her body on top of him added to the mix, and when she reached down to free his cock from his jeans, he thought he was about to burst. Sliding his hands along her thighs, Clint gathered up her skirts into a bunch and moved them behind her. They draped down to the floor, leaving her naked body revealed to him from the waist down.

Her blouse hung open to display her firm, pert breasts, which stood at attention, complete with small, pink nipples. Clint liked the way her clothes hung off of her; not completely on but not completely off. They were either pulled open or pushed to one side, making her nudity like a gift that was meant only for his eyes.

Clint's eyes roamed down her body, past her breasts and down over her flat stomach. She was still breathing heavily, her hands working furiously on his cock, stroking it up and down. Leaning back slightly, Clint took in the sight of her bare pussy. It was damp with moisture, slender pink lips glistening beneath the thatch of hair.

All he had to do was put his hands on her hips and pull

her closer for her to respond. Quickly, almost gratefully, she lifted herself up slightly and positioned his penis between her legs. Her wet lips fit perfectly over the tip of his cock and when she lowered down again, he slid into her inch by inch.

They both let out deep breaths as she gently took him inside of her. By the time he was all the way in, her body was trembling slightly once again. Joan's eyes opened and locked onto Clint. Her hands slipped around the back of his neck and clasped together to give her an anchor as she started riding up and down on his cock.

Clint still felt the occasional bit of dizziness from his wounds. At this moment, however, the subtle spinning sensation only added to the pleasure. It felt to him as if his chair was slowly tumbling through space while Joan bounced up and down in his lap.

After a few moments, they developed a perfect rhythm. She would grind her hips back and forth while riding him and Clint would pump up every now and then to add that extra groan in the back of her throat. No words passed between them, simply because none were needed. Their bodies were doing plenty of talking.

In fact, their bodies wound up having plenty of conversations before they were through.

FORTY-ONE

To say the courthouse in Origin was grand would have
been an understatement. However, despite all the fineries
embedded in the stone and woodwork, there was no doubt
as to what that courthouse truly was. It was a shrine, pure
and simple, but not a shrine to justice.

It was a shrine to Judge Henry Krueger.

There were plenty of courtrooms in the building where
plenty of trials took place presided over by a few other
judges. None of those rooms could compare to the one and
only courtroom that came close to matching the rest of the
building.

All of the other courtrooms were simple affairs of
wooden walls and solid tables. Whatever space was left
was taken up by dozens of chairs. The air was stuffy and
full of dust, billowing outward like a dirty wave from each
pound of the gavel.

Judge Krueger's courtroom, on the other hand, was no
such animal.

Judge Krueger's courtroom was just as grand as the
building surrounding it, with enough chairs to accommodate a trial double the size of any other courtroom. The ta-

bles were inlaid with stone and the jury box was more like the section for a choir.

Of course, the only thing to overshadow all of this was the bench where Judge Krueger sat. That bench resembled something from a painting of ancient Greece and was almost high enough to make Krueger seem like one of the Olympian gods.

Two days had passed since Clint had opened his eyes after the beating he'd gotten, and Krueger's courtroom was full to bursting. Every one of the numerous seats was filled and every bit of leftover space was filled by folks standing shoulder to shoulder just to bear witness to what was going on.

None of the people there looked interested or even curious as to how the trial would go. Instead, every face was sorrowful. There was also a certain surety in everyone's eyes, as though they'd already skipped ahead to the last page in a book.

They all knew what was going to happen.

It was just a matter of getting one last look at the accused before he was hauled off and never seen again, like so many others before him.

Two people sat at the defendant's table: one man and one woman. Neither of them looked overly anxious. Instead, they had the grim sort of peace in their eyes only seen when the ax was already speeding down on its way toward someone's neck.

They knew what was going to happen as well. Things had simply progressed so far that they saw no possible way out.

The lawyers had said their pieces and gone through their motions. That part of the proceedings was more or less a joke, because it was the judge and the judge alone who decided what would be done. The jury was a formality. Actually, they were just the part of the audience with the best seats in the house.

"Melinda Streeway," Krueger pronounced. "Rise and accept your judgment."

Misty hadn't gone by her proper name for so long that she barely recognized it. The way Krueger's eyes fixed on her was more than enough, however, to get her to comply to the command. The blonde rose from where she was sitting and stood with her hands clasped in front of her.

"You've been charged with associating with a known killer and conspiring to evade justice in this jurisdiction," Krueger said.

"I spent time with Clint Adams and left town when one of your own hired gunhands was trying to force himself on me," she spat back. "There's nothing wrong with that!"

Although she got plenty of approving nods from the audience, nobody dared to speak out in her favor.

"You've had your trial and the time to make your argument is passed."

"This ain't a trial. It's not even half a trial!"

"Miss Streeway, unless you want to add contempt to the list of your crimes, I suggest you shut your mouth."

"Or what?" she asked challengingly. "You'll hang me?"

Krueger's eyes were fixed intently upon her and he let a few moments pass before responding. "Are you finished?" He waited a bit more and nodded when he saw Misty lower her head in defeat. "Then I pronounce you guilty. You'll be taken from this courtroom immediately and then shipped to a proper facility to serve your sentence."

Several other dancers from the Neapolitan that were in the audience broke into tears and reached out for Misty as she was dragged out of the room by Wilde. The young gunhand was dressed in a clean set of black clothes and pushed Misty past her friends without letting her get in so much as one good-bye.

"That leaves you, Mr. Shoemaker," Krueger said, eyeing Mick with no small amount of self-satisfaction. "You were already charged and have since fled from custody. The appropriate additions will be made to your sentence and will be carried out immediately."

Although none of the audience knew exactly what additions Krueger was talking about, they all shuddered at the many gruesome possibilities.

"Take this piece of trash out of my sight."

Hearing that command from Judge Krueger, Deke and Marcus took hold of Mick by the arms and ushered him out. Mick hadn't said a word the entire time and he didn't say a word now. He knew whatever he might say would just be a waste of breath. As far as he was concerned, his last bit of hope had been snuffed out a few nights before.

"Now," Krueger said as the doors slammed shut behind the two condemned prisoners. "On to town business. The proposition has been made to elect myself as head of Origin's Town Council. As such, I would also assume the role of head justice for this county. Since we have most everyone here who would normally cast a vote in such matters, I'd like to hold a quick census."

There were confused glances as well as a few burning stares cast toward the judge's bench. Indeed, every member of the council was present, along with every other valued businessman in the community.

"All those opposed, speak up now," Krueger ordered.

With the shadow of the trial still hanging over their heads, not one person in that room had the strength to say a word. They were too busy wondering who might get singled out to die at the behest of the monster sitting upon his throne at the front of the room.

Krueger smiled. "Very well then. I'll assume my new duties immediately."

FORTY-TWO

Deke and his men rode out of town with one horse in tow. Both prisoners were tied to the saddle and bound so tightly that they couldn't move more than one muscle at a time. They rode to a familiar spot, although it was a spot they hadn't been to for a little while. The last time they'd hung someone there, it was summer and the trees were in full bloom. Now the branches were half-bare and the land itself felt dead.

Unfortunately, before too much longer, there was going to be a little more death on the landscape.

The prisoners didn't struggle. They didn't try to scream. They'd seen too many others lose the same struggle for them to think it could turn out any different this time around.

Deke rode up front. Wilde rode in the middle with the spare horse's reins in hand, while Marcus brought up the rear. Everyone in the group was calmly resigned to his or her fate, and all that remained was to carry out the task at hand. Everyone seemed almost content.

Everyone, that is, except for Marcus.

Something had been bothering him throughout the latter portion of the ride. It started with a strange feeling as they left town and continued to grow as they got closer to their destination. The cluster of old trees lay less than a mile ahead and could be seen like a blemish on the otherwise flat skyline. Rather than watch those trees get closer, he kept turning in his saddle to look behind.

Every time he turned around, Marcus swore he was going to catch sight of whatever it was that had been bothering him like a fly buzzing just outside of his field of vision. Sometimes he thought he heard something, and other times he thought he saw something. Not one of those times gave him something solid to work with, and each only added to a growing sense of frustration.

They arrived at the trees without incident. Acting without having to think about what he was doing, Deke swung down from his horse and retrieved the rope that had been hanging from his saddle. He fashioned the lengths of rope into two nooses, his hands working of their own accord.

"What's the matter, Marcus?" Deke asked. "You look like something's got you spooked."

Still in his saddle, Marcus flashed his eyes toward Deke and snapped, "I ain't spooked."

"You could've fooled me," Deke said with a smirk.

"I thought there was something out here, is all."

Wilde had his eyes fixed on the prisoners as he climbed down from his horse and checked their bonds. "They say that ghosts come up in places where lots of folks were killed. I'd say this place qualifies."

"Shut up, Wilde," Deke growled. "We don't have time for that bullshit. Do you think there's someone out there or not, Marcus?"

Being the tracker of the group, Marcus cast his eyes slowly around. Not only was he looking for signs of movement, but he was listening for anything as well. Judging by the way he lifted his face to every incoming breeze, one might have thought he was even tasting the air. Finally, he shrugged. "Could be."

Having finished the first noose, Deke tossed it up and over one of the thick branches of the biggest tree. "If there is, it's too late for an ambush. They'll have to come to us and that's just fine by me."

"You think it may be Adams?" Wilde asked.

Marcus was staring at a clump of shrubs less than a quarter mile away. "Adams is dead."

"We don't know that for sure," Wilde said. "He was hurt, but we didn't actually see for sure that he was killed."

"If Adams is alive," Deke said, "he's not a threat to us. We took care of him once and we can do it again. After the way we locked horns before, I'd welcome another chance at him. I don't much care for sloppy wins like that one."

"A kill's a kill," Marcus said without taking his eyes from the spot he'd been studying. A second later, he spotted another glimpse of motion coming from another direction. Now that he was looking around, he was picking out plenty of other clumps of trees that he hadn't paid much attention to in the past.

Any one of those clumps could have hidden a single horse. In fact, thinking back on it, Marcus even thought of plenty of other similar hiding places along the way.

"Talk to me, Marcus," Deke said. "You look like you just heard some mighty bad news."

"I'm not sure yet, but there might be someone else around here."

No more than a few seconds after those words trailed off, the wind shifted and all three men caught a familiar sound. It was the sound of hooves pounding against the earth, and they were coming fast.

"What's that?" Wilde asked, his hand instinctively going toward his holster.

For the first time since they'd been tied to their horse, both prisoners lifted their eyes to look around. Misty was already wearing an optimistic smile, but Mick was being a bit more cautious. She turned around to look at him and spoke in an excited whisper.

"He's coming," she said. "I know it."

Wilde reached up and smacked Mick on the back of the head even though he wasn't the one who'd spoken. "What're you saying? Tell me!"

Before Mick could say anything in reply, all five of them spotted a figure that had skylined itself ahead. The shape was definitely that of a man on horseback, with so much dirt being kicked up behind him that he must have been riding faster than the wind.

Deke calmly walked around his horse to get to the rifle hanging from the saddle. "Get ready," he said to his men.

The figure in the distance stopped just outside of rifle range and straightened up to announce himself even more. When he shouted toward the group under the trees, the wind carried the figure's voice along like the howl of some kind of angry spirit.

"Let them go," the figure said.

"Jesus Lord Almighty," Deke said, squinting at the figure. "I can't believe it. It's Adams."

FORTY-THREE

When Joan had taken Clint to the stable where she'd moved Eclipse, he swore that horse was one of the prettiest sights he'd seen in a long time. The Darley Arabian stallion was already anxiously pacing in his stall, but when he saw Clint he practically kicked down the gate.

Seeing Eclipse again meant more to Clint than just checking in with an old friend. It meant that there was indeed some hope to pull this whole situation out of the fire after all. Joan had kept him up-to-date on what was happening with the bogus double trial being held in Judge Krueger's courtroom.

That trial was nothing but Krueger flexing his muscles and striking back at the two people who'd dared to choose the wrong side in a fight. When he'd heard about it, Clint's first instinct was to bust in during the proceedings and put a stop to the farce before the inevitable verdict was handed down.

Joan had practically cried when she saw him tense and start to head out the door. "There's too many men there," she said.

"Only a few of them will stand against me" was Clint's response.

"They're waiting for you. Those gunmen, I mean. Even though you killed one of them, that'll just make the others want to shoot you down even worse."

"That'll make them sloppy."

"Maybe they won't shoot you first, Clint. Did you think about that?"

Clint had stopped when he heard that. His hand was on the door and he was a heartbeat from stepping outside. He didn't need to read those books in Krueger's chambers and he didn't need to hear any more testimony for himself. As far as he was concerned, Krueger and his men had shown what they were truly made of and had done a fine job of proving Mick's stories to be true.

At the very least, Krueger was a bloodthirsty maniac who took pride in condemning innocent people to death just because he had his own ambitions. At the very worst, the judge was capable of becoming a bloodthirsty maniac with an entire political machine at his fingertips.

Krueger had to be stopped.

Clint knew that above all else.

But what would Krueger do to keep from going under? Would he take hostages or have even more innocents thrown between himself and Clint's modified Colt? It certainly wasn't beyond him.

All the particulars no longer mattered. It didn't matter who Krueger was or what he did for a living. It didn't matter what his reasons were or what he hoped to become. All that did matter was what Krueger had done and the bodies he'd left behind.

All of Clint's doubts had been taken away when he was hiding under that cot and heard Deke talking so openly about the judge's intents. More people were going to die if nothing was done about it, and that was more than enough to put the steam in Clint's stride.

"They'll kill you," Joan said while reaching out to touch Clint's arm.

Clint took hold of her hand, pulled her in closer and planted a kiss on her lips that made the next several minutes melt away. When they parted, they kept their eyes fixed on each other.

"They already tried killing me. It didn't work out too well. Now they're set to kill plenty of others," Clint said. "That's why I've got to go after them."

She watched as he collected his gear and pulled on his coat. "You're not coming back," she whispered. "Even if you don't get another scratch from them, you're not coming back, are you?"

Clint turned to look at her once again and lowered his eyes before saying another word. "Thanks for all you've done. If there's any way for me to repay you . . ."

"You want to repay me?" Joan asked, rearing up with renewed strength. "Make sure that son of a bitch killer doesn't come back to rape this town any more. That's a way to repay everyone in Origin, as well as plenty of other towns."

Clint nodded to her, tipped his hat and left. In that moment, the promise was made.

She let him go, still wishing she could convince him to pick any other direction in which to ride.

After that, it had been a simple matter of getting himself ready to move without being seen until the time was right. With all that was happening in town with the trial and all, that wasn't half as difficult as it may have seemed.

Clint kept out of sight with his eyes peeled and his hand never far from his Colt. As much as he wanted to bust up that trial, he held back just to keep all those innocent bystanders out of harm's way. The next time he ran into the remaining Horsemen, Clint knew it was going to get bloody. It certainly wouldn't be a proper place for anyone not ready for war.

The prisoners were brought out and loaded onto their horses, giving Clint just enough time to run and fetch

Eclipse so he could follow them. Any other tracker might not have been able to pick up Deke's trail, and any other horse might not have been fast enough to actually get ahead of it.

Once he knew what direction the horsemen were headed, Clint merely had to race ahead of them and stay there. Once the group came to a stop in those trees, he snuck up as close as he could get before it was time to show himself. When that time came, he rode Eclipse to the closest rise and made sure to make his silhouette stick out like a sore thumb. Clint could see everyone in those trees come to a stop, which was when he shouted out his single demand.

"Let them go!" he roared.

Nobody moved right away. They were all too busy talking and planning among themselves.

Clint wasn't about to wait for them one more second. He drew his rifle from the holster on Eclipse's saddle and snapped the reins. Pressing the rifle against his shoulder, Clint steadied himself as best he could on top of the racing stallion and squeezed off the first shot.

FORTY-FOUR

"Holy shit!" was all Wilde managed to say when he saw the puff of smoke come from Clint's rifle.

That was all that could be seen from that distance, and it was a second or two before the hiss of lead speeding through the air was followed by the crack of gunfire. The three gunmen ducked low and got their own weapons ready, leaving the prisoners out in the open.

Clint's shot went well over everyone's head, and for a moment it seemed as though he'd missed whatever he'd been aiming at. Nobody there would have held poor marksmanship against him. Not at that distance. But when the noose dropped from the tree where it had been cut cleanly by the bullet, it was clear Clint hadn't missed anything.

Deke gritted his teeth and shook his head. "Son of a bitch," he grumbled. "Why can't this bastard stay dead?"

Eclipse's hooves rumbled like an approaching storm.

Marcus tried to get a look at Clint, but was forced to drop back down again by another shot from Clint's rifle. That shot was followed by another and then another, each bullet kicking up dirt only a few inches from where each gunman was hiding. None of those bullets drew blood, but

177

they served to keep Deke and his men from sticking their necks out.

One more shot cut through the air. This one wasn't aimed at any of the gunmen, but it did draw a trickle of blood. The lead hissed through the air and clipped the flank of the horse carrying both prisoners on its back. That shot was the equivalent of a smack on the rump and got the horse scurrying away from the cluster of trees.

Deke looked around at his men. Each of them had his back pressed against a tree, just as he did. They couldn't do much to stop the horse from carrying their prisoners away. Trying to gun the prisoners down would have wasted valuable ammunition, and reaching out for the reins would have been suicide.

So, as much as he hated to do it, Deke simply let the horse go. He figured it would be a simple enough matter to gather the prisoners up once Adams was done for good. Of course, there was one mighty big job to accomplish before he worried about collecting any horse.

"Here he comes," Marcus said as the rumble of hooves got closer.

Each of the others nodded to signal he was ready to make his move. The sound of the oncoming horse was unmistakable and obviously galloping in on their left. They steeled themselves and readied their weapons as the Darley Arabian thundered through the cluster of trees.

Moving like the well-oiled machine they were, all three of the gunmen jumped out from their cover just in time to get a good shot at whoever was riding on the stallion's back. Of course, the only flaw in their plan was that nobody was riding on Eclipse's back.

Clint had leapt from his saddle before getting into the trees, and had moved around to approach the gunmen on their right. He knew they wouldn't be fooled long by the ruse, but Clint didn't exactly need much time to gain the edge he was after.

Letting out a sharp whistle, he squared his shoulders to where Wilde was standing and hefted his rifle over his left shoulder. The youngest of the gunmen spun around and lifted his gun to fire.

Clint let the kid move just far enough to commit himself before drawing the Colt from its holster. His hand flashed so quickly that it could hardly be seen. There was a flicker of motion, the glint of steel being bared and then the flash of gunfire.

The Colt spat out a single round through a gout of smoke and fire. That round sliced through the air to drill a clean hole into Wilde's chest and a rather messy one on its way out.

Wilde let out a surprised grunt as he was lifted from his feet. His finger clenched around his trigger, but it was only a reflexive action and that bullet buried itself into a tree next to where Clint had been standing. He wasn't standing there anymore, however, which was why the return fire from Deke and Marcus hit nothing but smoke-filled air.

As Wilde's body dropped, the remaining two gunmen were fanning out from their positions. With Clint standing only a few yards away, there was nowhere left to hide and no point in trying to run. Neither man bothered looking to see what the other was doing. Marcus and Deke had fought enough side-by-side that they could guess exactly what each other had in mind.

Clint kept his eyes darting between the two, knowing full well that they were the only ones left. Even if Deke had any other men, Clint had watched them for long enough to know that nobody else had followed them out of Origin.

The next couple of seconds were vital. It was a moment that happened many times in the middle of a shoot-out, where there was a slight calm in the storm. Deke and Marcus weren't firing, because they knew that would only make them the next target. Clint wasn't about to shift his aim to one of them, because that would free up the other.

It was a tense standoff, and none of the men in the fight was stupid enough to be the one to break it.

Fortunately, it didn't take a man to move things along.

Suddenly, the ground shook behind Marcus's feet as a massive impact slammed within inches of him. The impact was caused by Eclipse's hooves as the horse reared up and came back down again behind the gunman. The Darley Arabian wasn't the kind of animal to be spooked by gunfire and would respond to Clint's whistle even if it meant charging straight into the fray.

This was one of those times, and Clint couldn't have been more grateful.

Feeling the closeness of the angry horse forced Marcus's hand and rushed him into making the next move. If only to get away from Eclipse, Marcus ducked down low and ran to one side, taking a shot at Clint as he went.

The bullet came close, but Clint managed to drop to one knee just in time to let the lead cut through the air inches from him. Before his knee hit the ground, Clint answered with a shot of his own that caught Marcus in the shoulder and spun him around.

Marcus landed on his side and immediately propped himself up on one elbow. From there, he struggled to lift his revolver so he could sight down its barrel.

In this time, Deke had gotten himself behind the closest tree he could find and was leaning around to take a shot at Clint. He managed to squeeze off a shot, but he was in too much of a hurry to gain any kind of accuracy.

Since there wasn't much cover to be had, Clint did the only thing he could: He stayed low and kept his wits about him even as the bullets threatened to end his life at any given second.

Clint winced as one of Deke's shots grazed his neck and went screaming into the air behind him. At that same moment, Marcus narrowed his eyes and began tightening his grip on his trigger. Extending his hand and pointing the

Colt as he would point his own finger, Clint fired a single shot which blew Marcus's right eye clean through the back of his skull.

"You can't save them, Adams!" Deke hollered as he pressed his back against the tree and shifted his aim to the prisoners cowering nearby. "I came here to kill these two and I'm gonna do it. Even if it's just to spit in your face I'm gonna—"

Three shots exploded through the air. They came in quick succession from Clint's modified Colt and were followed by the sound of lead tunneling through wood. Three holes were blasted through the tree Deke was using as cover, and when Deke slumped forward, he had two holes through his spine.

FORTY-FIVE

Clint rode into town with Misty and Mick riding right with him. The other horses were following as well, but the men strapped across their backs weren't in as good shape. The group was spotted immediately, and locals came rushing out from every storefront and every house to follow them as they rode straight up to the courthouse steps.

Judge Krueger emerged from his courthouse like a king from his palace and gazed down at the crowd spread out before him. Practically the entire town was gathered there, but Krueger still managed to look down his nose at each and every one of them.

"What's going on here?" Krueger bellowed.

Clint came forward, bringing the horses bearing their dead riders with him. "I just came to bring your men back to you," he said.

There was an audible gasp when the crowd saw for certain that the bodies really were those of the judge's feared gunmen. When Krueger saw them, the wince on his face was just pronounced enough for everyone to see.

"You . . . you're a murderer," Krueger said, trying to maintain his composure.

Clint shook his head. "I was defending myself as well as

these two people who everyone here knows are innocent."

"I pronounced my judgment."

"Your word isn't worth shit!" It wasn't Clint who said that, but one of the locals who were stepping forward toward the stairs.

"Yeah," said another man, who walked straight past Clint and toward Krueger. "You're the killer here."

Krueger stopped trying to keep up his appearances. He was getting scared and there was no way for him to hide it. "I'm the head of the Town Council. I'm a judge, for Christ's sake!"

But with his enforcers laying dead in the street, the judge's threats no longer had teeth. Clint watched as more and more of the locals stepped forward to take hold of Krueger and start dragging him toward the gallows that had gone unused for the last several months.

"What are you doing?" Krueger shouted. "This isn't right! What's happening?" Looking to Clint, the judge became desperate and started struggling against the dozens of grips moving him along. "What is this!?"

But Clint wasn't listening. He was already riding out of town.

"This," Mick said after giving Clint one last, grateful wave, "is justice."

Watch for

DEATH IN DENVER

the 279th novel in the exciting GUNSMITH
series from Jove

Coming in March!

J. R. ROBERTS

THE GUNSMITH

GIANT ACTION! GIANT ADVENTURE!

THE GUNSMITH

GIANT

GIANT WESTERNS FEATURING THE GUNSMITH

**AVAILABLE WHEREVER BOOKS ARE SOLD OR AT
WWW.PENGUIN.COM**

J799

**Explore the exciting Old West with one
of the men who made it wild!**

JAKE LOGAN
TODAY'S HOTTEST ACTION WESTERN!